TRANSFER TO YESTERDAY

TRANSFER TO YESTERDAY

ISIDORE HAIBLUM

DOUBLEDAY & COMPANY, INC.

GARDEN CITY, NEW YORK

1981

The future world consists of a host of
warring factions, each devoted to its
own kind of "truth," and a man from
another dimension possesses a secret
that could destroy the world.

ISBN: 0-385-17136-6
Library of Congress Catalog Card Number: 80-2248
Copyright © 1973 by Isidore Haiblum
All Rights Reserved
Printed in the United States of America

PROLOGUE

The man with the gun leaned forward in his chair. Medium height. Smooth, even features. Neatly-trimmed black hair, slicked back, parted on the left. His smile, when he used it, wasn't especially mirthful. "Listen," he said, his voice surprisingly flat, holding the faintest edge of impatience.

The room was dark. Light spilled through a half-opened window —a winking red neon glare touting the chophouse downstairs and the paler glow of street lamps out on the pavement below. Cars went by. The flaking bars of a fire escape clung to the window like a rejected lover's embrace. An el tunneled along somewhere through the night and a lone foghorn crooned its dirge over the waterfront.

"Sure, Eddy," the other man said. "Anything you say, Eddy; just name it." This other man, perched on a three-legged stool in the far corner, kept fidgeting; shadows covered him like jittering black drapes.

"I'm going to tell you once," the man with the gun said, "and no more. You listen."

"Look, Eddy, how come the rod? I kicked in plenty, didn't I? Hell, there ain't nothing left. You know that. I'm down two grand—"

"Stow it."

Both men were silent.

"You hear me?" the man with the gun said presently.

"I hear you."

"Then clam up. Maybe you'll learn something. You already know part of it, but I'm giving you the rest."

"Well, that's fine . . ."

"Maybe. We'll see."

NORTON ONE

THE WILDERNESS

So far, so good. Holding my own at least. I came over the rise chewing up the terrain, but I was dead on my feet, a walking wash-out. Somewhere along the line I'd lost the stun gun; that made it worse.

I was stuck out here in the middle of nowhere.

An early morning sun cut through white, scudding clouds. A wide slice of blue sky showing. The wind rose.

I saw the city.

From where I stood it might have been a scale model, the towers and steeples gem-like, light slanting off steel and glass. It was undeniably something; it looked pretty as a painted think-tape.

An illusion. Distance had lent it a false veneer. In essence the city was as charming as a backwoods privy, but comparisons were hard to come by. There was nothing at hand to match it against.

I was mildly surprised to see that I'd gotten this far. I hadn't expected it. But I was still too far away. Prospects had a decidedly gloomy look. Too much territory lay between me and that city, too much trouble.

"You want something, anny?"

That was the keep. The outposter. He'd stepped out of his bungalow to greet me.

"A ride," I said.

Dull, hazel eyes examined me. The man frowned as if he didn't quite like what he saw. "Where to?" His voice had the texture of chalk grating against a blackboard. He'd never make the church choir. But then, there weren't any churches left either.

"The city," I told him.

His clean-shaven head bobbed like a piece of refuse in a sewer pipe. The eyes were glaring now. "Not me, anny," he almost spat.

I'd hit a responsive chord. He'd come alive. It was hardly an improvement.

"Look—" I began.

"Forget it, anny."

Those eyes bothered me. I recognized the signs. Doped up. A nodhooker's eyes. He'd need it to stay sane out here in the wilds. Only, sanity wasn't that much of an asset for an outposter. I had a feeling that he'd never see reason, that he'd been conditioned against it. I had to try anyway.

"Come on," I said, "we're both annys," as if that meant anything. It didn't. *Anny*—with a small *a*—an overworked term that'd knocked out *citizen*. A citizen, history had it, was a person who owed allegiance to a government, was entitled to its protection. But when government went by the boards, even the squarest citizen became, willy-nilly, an anarchist. And protection only meant toeing the line.

"Anny"—with a capital A—was something else, a corruption of *Anschluss*, a crazy quilt of special-interest groups that had formed when government had folded. Competing groups. All-encompassing life-groups. Annys. A legacy from the good old days.

The Annys had scant contact with one another; they didn't get along with each other one bit. Only the H computer linked them all. No one liked a heretic, and all the Annys wanted to be certain that none turned up on their turf. It didn't matter what a glink believed; if he'd shucked the line once, he might do it again. No one wanted to take the risk; it could be catching. And protection only meant toeing the line.

I went on—putting reasonableness in my voice. "There ought to be some way two adult annys can settle—"

"You read, anny?"

"Read?" That caught me by surprise. Of course, a lot of annys didn't. "Sure," I said. "Actually, I'm a professor at—"

"See the logo?"

I nodded. Unfortunately, I'd seen it.

"Look again."

I looked again.

ASSOCIATION

I could have done without it. It hung there like some obscene chunk of graffiti over the small, white, *armored* bungalow door. And what it spelled out was fini for poor old James N. Norton, ex-professor of League history. Well, you can't win them all. But it's nice, every now and then, to at least make a good showing.

"Want me rotting in the tombs?" the outposter wanted to know, matter-of-factly, as though he were asking about going fishing. Good old nod, it was doing its stuff again, what it was cut out to do. The outposter was all composure again. An earthquake might ruffle his feathers some, but then there was always another shot of happiness. "No sir," he said smartly. "No Association standard in the city. How you figure on getting around *that?*"

An oversight, all right. I tried a different tack. "To the borders only," I said with feeling. "I can pay. Index is no problem." Index was accepted inter-Anny currency these days. Which meant you just might get by with it in most parts of the city—if you had lots of luck and knew the right annys. Otherwise, there was always food or clothing to trade. Even old socks. The barter market was a going concern.

The outposter gave me his answer, a good one. "Who's going to ride escort?"

"I will!" Only it came out too much a question. I didn't think the keep could drive and shoot at the same time, and there'd be no one else around. But would he buy it?

"Don't trust you," he said simply.

I couldn't blame him. Trust was a one-way ticket to tombstone row. A loser's proposition.

The outposter said, "Pretty short on the think, aren't you, anny?"

I had to admit it, I was off the think by miles.

He sighed. "Hell, I'm as human as the next glink; I'm no sloot, anny, but we've all got different standards. I'm Association. You're what?"

"League."

"Well, there you are. I wouldn't trust a Leaguer."

"Whom would you trust?"

"No one. What're you doing out here, anyway?"

"An accident."

"The usual," he sneered.

"My car overturned."

"The others?"

"None. I was alone."

He stared at me as if I'd sprouted tusks and he was wondering to what zoo I ought to be committed. We were both silent now. A bird cooed. Crickets. Wind combing weeds, bushes, grass. The sun was glinting off the keep's bald pate as if he were sending special signals to some hidden place in the woods. Perhaps he was. "All right," he finally spoke, "you had an accident. You in good standing?"

Sure. *Unless I'd already been posted.* "Of course," I said.

He shrugged. "The best I can offer you, anny, is shelter."

So it'd come down to *that.* Too bad—it wasn't quite best enough.

But it did prove something:

Under it all—the think-tape exposures, the conditioning—this glink was still half-way human. But that wasn't good enough either.

Once in the bungalow, I'd have to submit:

The H check.

H for heretic.

H for me.

And even if they didn't have my number yet, if I stayed, waited around for rescue, sooner or later it'd turn up.

I had another idea:

Perhaps I could call ahead, warn Nina and Brent. A call-box on the premises?

Even that was beyond my reach. Association was outzone, no hook-up with League numbers.

I said, "Sorry. Shelter's no good. I've got business in the city; it can't wait."

"You're making a mistake, anny. You'll never get there, not on foot."

That was no news. And there was nothing I could do about it.

Except kill him.

A garage lay behind the bungalow. A vehicle would be in it. I could run the roads and take my chances. If I could get that car.

Some chance.

A laser hung on the keep's hip. I was unarmed, as empty-handed as a wailing toddler.

Standing six-one, I was pretty tall for these parts. In this outposter, though, they'd picked a giant. Six-six if anything. A rock.

And the outpost itself made the whole point academic.

One false move from the ragged stranger who claimed to be a Leaguer in *good standing* and the bungalow would cut loose, would trigger an eruption of violence that'd reduce said stranger—instantly —to a tiny smoldering ash heap. No more, no less.

So much for heroics.

The doctrine of *Safe Conduct* had smoothed my way with this glink. As long as I didn't enter his precious bungalow he wouldn't push me. Etiquette still counted for something.

But it couldn't help me here.

I turned to go.

"Anny!"

I stood rooted. "What?"

I didn't think he was going to change his mind. He didn't.

"Sloots," he said. "You can't go that way."

"It's a free wilderness," I reminded him. I showed him my back and stalked away. I was tired of talking. One last glimpse of the towers:

League gold.

Federation blue.

Alliance green.

Coalition brown.

Corporation silver . . .

Hundreds of them.

Then I was back in the jungle, the city gone. I was alone.

The wind grew stronger.

I kept going, making my way around trees, vines, branches, over loose earth.

Early autumn.

A blaze of drying leaves on the ground. Sunlight flicked through the foliage, bounced off the trees like a cardsharp giving a wide shuffle. An animal hooted somewhere. Birds. Things scurried through the underbrush.

Rain had come last night. Here the ground was only damp. I smelled earth, leaves, grass. The wind bent the branches back.

After a while I rested.

Touch and go. My survival was nothing to bet on. *Believe in lost causes, anny?*

I looked around.

The crooked street sign said:

96th Street, Madison Avenue.

An artifact from another era. Of course, people had once lived here, had called themselves citizens. Another world. *Or was it?*

Streets.

Businesses.

Dwellings.

Schools.

Stores.

Markets.

I'd seen the ancient maps, texts, even photographs. I'd been one of the few. But could I believe it? Did I have a choice? Did it matter? Probably not. That was the truth. It just didn't matter any more. And yet I kept wondering. To the eye of the trained historian —even Anny-trained—the gaps were patently obvious.

Planned error?

It might be. Why not? The Lacers, our top of the heap, could have "corrected" the files in the documents chamber at will. Nothing would have been simpler. Only the historians might grumble—secretly, to be sure—and they were hardly paid for veracity.

There was no way to know.

Probably, this had once been an urban center. All the texts I'd read—hundreds of them—pointed that way, backed each other up. It was really something when a man begins to doubt his own senses. Put it down to bad company; my environment had left something to be desired . . .

The traces were all here around me.

Ruins of buildings.

Blocks of chipped pavement.

A battered lamp and street sign.

And underneath—no doubt—the collapsed subway tunnels, sewer systems, utility lines . . .

Not a jungle. Not in the ordinary sense.

It lacked a prerequisite.

Beasts of prey.

But then it had something else.

FLEISHER ONE

AFTER THE SWAG

Eddy Fleisher lay back, stretched out on his narrow bunk like some embalmed stiff, not moving at all, the fake Indian blanket with its black triangles and squares itching just a little bit, hands tucked behind his head. In the next room the faucet went drip-drop, sounding like: *wanna buy a duck?* It was getting on his nerves. He wondered idly if something had gone wrong.

Six o'clock came and went.

There was always the radio for chit-chat. Some choice: Uncle Don, Buck Rogers, or the U. S. Army band.

He'd already breezed through the afternoon sheets: *The World Telegram, The Sun, The Post, The Evening American.* Nothing else in the whole joint. He had failed to provide for his leisure hours. It was a failing he shared with ten million others, only he was working and they weren't. It made a difference.

6:30 offered news. Eddy Fleisher restrained himself; it was bound to be rotten. He hummed a few bars of Teagarden's *I Got a Right to Sing the Blues*. Last year's ditty, but not old hat; not for him, not for anyone. No such luck, buddy. He got up and poured out a hooker of gin, hesitated, then neatly poured it back down the bottle. He'd licked the booze for this hand—had chucked it—it made sense to keep it that way. Eddy Fleisher went back to his cot.

He clicked on the set for Amos 'n' Andy at 7:00. Swinging the dial to WOR at 7:15 he gave Lum and Abner a whirl.

Every little while the Ninth Avenue el screamed a greeting into his flat: stink and holler on the run. He was camped on the third floor of a walk-up and the tracks made straight lines past his windows. Dusk filtered through the off-white gauze curtains, lengthened the already long shadows on the walls. A tug hooted somewhere down by the waterfront; horns honked on the street below. He could hear the crippled newsie on the corner of 39th Street hawking away —the early *News* and *Mirror*. He couldn't make out the words.

7:30: the Easy Aces came on on WEAF. 7:45: he gave Boake Carter the ear. The news was even worse than he'd figured. Kansas was blowing away. The Sahara Desert had come to roost in the US of A. At least "Dust Bowl" sounded poetic. Hitler had a new draft plan and was telling the Reichstag about it. Huey Long was going to run for President. It got dark. A warm glow came from the radio's dial light. Eddy Fleisher lit a Camel. Above him on the fourth floor a lot of romping was going on. The guy up there was an out-of-work printer who'd become an out-and-out bum; he showed how far you can go on a bread line; his missus and three kids were still dragging along. Only, to Fleisher's way of thinking, there wasn't much promise in it. The water pipe in the kitchen seemed to be burping up a small squall. One window was open and Fleisher could hear voices arguing shrilly out on the street. He turned over on his left side. 8:00 brought the Lone Ranger to WOR. Fleisher passed it by.

Rousing himself at 9:00, he shuffled off into the kitchen and searched through the icebox. He scrambled some eggs, fried a couple of ham slices, set a coffee pot bubbling on the burner. Not quite the Ritz. The previous tenant had left a tinted photo of Roosevelt hanging on the wall. The President was grinning. The mess wasn't his fault, of course, but then he hadn't done a helluva lot to change things either. Maybe no one could. Eddy Fleisher didn't know.

He finished chow, rinsed dishes, dried hands, doused light, and ambled back to the bedroom. An el whooped by. Streetlights did things to his walls. The Eastman Orchestra fiddled away on WEAF. The evening looked like a dud. Eddy Fleisher began to doze.

Loud knuckles rapped on his door. Prying open an eyelid, Fleisher held his wristwatch close to the radio's dial light: 11:15. He killed the music, swung off the bed. "Yeah?" he said at the door.

"For Pete's sake," a voice whispered. "Lemme in. It's me. Tom."

Eddy Fleisher unlocked the door.

A tall bird with a pointy nose, cleft chin, sallow complexion, loose tweed overcoat, and soft-brimmed gray hat swept by as if the forty thieves were at his heels.

"Christ," he told Eddy Fleisher, "close it." The hall was empty. Eddy Fleisher closed it.

"Lock it," the voice said in the darkness.

"You sound lousy," Eddy Fleisher said, and locked it. "What's the matter?"

"*Jesus*. You know what's happened?"

"I wouldn't be asking if I knew. Let's you and me go to the other room."

Making light in the kitchen, Eddy Fleisher nodded his visitor to a chair, uncapped a pint of scotch, planted himself across the table from Tom Lacy and said:

"Well? Spill it, brother."

Tom Lacy put hat on table, splashed whiskey into a glass, and belted it down. Wiping lips with the back of a hairy hand, he whispered:

"They copped Earl."

"You can talk," Eddy Fleisher told him. "The neighbors don't care. Who did?"

"The Kraft bunch."

Eddy Fleisher was interested. "Yeah?"

"Honest to God."

"H-m-m-m," Fleisher said, "that's not so bad. When?"

"A couple hours ago. Whaddya mean, not so bad? It's murder."
Lacy was using his chair like a hobby horse, rocking back and forth.

"Take it easy," Fleisher advised him.

Lacy tipped the whiskey bottle over his glass, poured, his eyes
worried.

Eddy Fleisher said:

"You don't want to get tanked up now, Tom. The law would've
been worse."

"Worse? Hell, they'll squeeze him."

"Maybe."

"Whaddya mean, maybe? There ain't no maybes."

"We can square it."

"Oh Jesus. You're cracked. Cut it out, Eddy. It gives me the
creeps to hear you, honest to God. Who's got that kind of dough?
Look, he don't know beans about you; you're clean. It's *me* he's
gonna finger. Oh Christ, they'll squeeze him. I gotta duck, hop a rattler or somethin'; only look, I'm busted flat, honest to God, that's
the truth. I put down my last cent on this kid Jackson—a lock, see?
This kid's got a sweet right; he can hook. And the other bum's a
bum. Only my guy went in the tank. I blew the whole roll. You
gotta help me."

Eddy Fleisher grinned at him.

"Don't be a sap, Tom."

"Huh?" Lacy's eyes jerked in their sockets like dice hitting a table,
stared at Fleisher.

"They'll nail you," Eddy Fleisher told him. "They'll come after
you, find you wherever you are. You can't hide from Kraft."

"Hell!"

"Uh-uh."

"I sure as hell can try!"

Fleisher shrugged. "Suit yourself."

"Aw . . . don't be that way, Eddy."

"I'm giving you the straight of it," Fleisher told him. "You can't
buck Kraft. It's a pipedream; you haven't got a prayer."

Tom Lacy waved a hand, almost knocking over the bottle.
"Baloney! What kind of talk is that? Look! Why should they want
me? I ain't got nothin'; Earl's got the stuff—"

"You don't get it," Eddy Fleisher said patiently. "Kraft's a vindictive bastard, that's why; it makes his shop look sick when some ghee nicks it and goes waltzing off—that's why. Even with an empty kick you're a loose end, Tom; and Kraft doesn't like loose ends; he'll find you."

"Jesus. What am I gonna do?"

"All this happened when?"

"I told you. A couple hours ago."

"You sure?"

"Sure I'm sure."

"Who gave it to you?"

"Clem. He was workin' the night shift, see? They hauled him right off in front of him."

"Okay. That's not so bad."

"There you go again."

"We still got time. Use your head."

Tom Lacy narrowed his eyes. "Time," he said, "for what?"

"To square it. To cut him loose."

"*That's* what you mean?"

"Yeah."

"Oh no! You're cracked! You really are."

"Pipe down," Eddy Fleisher said. "Leave that stuff for Paul Muni."

"No, I don't wanna hear no more. Christ. You're off your rocker, Eddy. I'm tellin' you, Earl's sunk; I gotta lam outta here. The best thing you can do—"

Eddy Fleisher said:

"That's the bunk. They haven't put the screws on him yet."

"Huh?"

"They haven't tumbled to you or anything. Stop sweating. We've got till morning."

"For Chrissakes, how do ya figure *that*?"

"Because I know Kraft, know how that crew works. I made it my business to know. They won't pump him till morning. They'll be holed up in the detention room of the plant, the northwest wing. They'll wait for Kraft to show—he gets a rear out of the rough stuff —and he doesn't move till after breakfast. That gives us maybe nine, ten hours. We can spring him, Tom. There won't be that many holding down the office. And I've still got the phony pass. We can get onto the grounds. From there it'll be duck soup, a cinch."

Lacy groaned again. "In a pig's eye it will. Oh, Jesus. What's *wrong* with you, Eddy?"

"The pair of us together, Tom, we can swing it. This way you won't even show in it. We pry him loose while he's still clammed up and we're home free. You're not going to sit still for your buddy taking a licking, are you?"

"Lay off, already. What're you kickin' about? You don't even know the bum. What's gotten into you, Eddy? I don't get it. You tired of breathin'? You *go* for bein' shot?"

Eddy Fleisher shrugged irritably.

"No one's shooting anyone. We can get him out without that. There're advantages. You don't get turned up, for one thing, and I don't have to sweat your spilling the works some day—that's another."

"Aw, come on, Eddy. You know me better'n that."

"I told you," Eddy Fleisher said, "Kraft won't give it up. If Earl goes, you're next, and then it's me. I'm not going to chance it."

"Jesus."

"Let's stop all this wrangling and get a move on. You're coming with me."

"Eddy, you don't know what you're askin'."

"I'm telling, not asking. They won't be expecting something like this. We can take 'em easy. All this shooting crap—that's a lot of hooey. You leave it to me."

"Look—you're so hot for this, you do it."

"Uh-uh," Fleisher said. "Don't be a chump, Tom; you're in, you're staying in."

"Why, for Pete's sake?"

"It's like this, Tom. I've put too much in this to see it go down the drain now. Earl doesn't know me. But he knows you. We're going to split the haul three ways: you, me, and Earl. He's got it stashed somewhere. So we need him. We pry him loose before he coughs up the goods for Kraft and then we split. Earl's got to know I'm in it and you're the Joe to tell him. He'll be grateful, all right,

when he sees what we've done for him. He'll come through.
And if he doesn't, we can do to him what Kraft would've done. I've
waited too long for my end of the cut. I'm going after it now. And
I'm not letting you gum it. I'm not letting Kraft gum it. You're
gonna hold up your end, Tom. That's flat!"

"So that's it," Lacy said. "You son-of-a-bitch. You're after the
swag."

"That's it," Eddy Fleisher said. "I'm after the swag."

NORTON TWO

THE OUTPOST

The worst of it, I knew, was that I'd been warned, warned often
enough. Yet some glinks—naming no names, of course—never take
advice. I had no one to blame but myself. And that wasn't worth
the effort.

I kissed her.
"No you don't," she said.
"I don't?"
"Answer my question." She pushed me away.
"It won't do any good," I said.
"Pardon me," a voice said.
I looked up to see the lady from the next dorm, a plump, short
woman who was discouragingly plain and in her fifties.
"Can you spare some meat?" she asked anxiously.
"Meat?"
"Chops? Hamburgers? Roast?"
"How's your father?" Nina asked.

The lady said fine.

"No," I said. "Where would we get that? Have you tried the powdered stuff? It's not bad this week."

The lady said no and went away.

Nina said, "There's half a lamb chop left."

"I know," I said. "I lied."

"You folks take the cake," Brent said. He was seated in the red and gold easy-seat.

Brent and I were colleagues in the League history banks. He was a chubby man in his mid-thirties whose cherubic, mustached face usually wore the friendly grin of a paid advocate. Which, in a sense, he was. We all were, from mid-echelon up. The system demanded it.

Brent said, "So you're really going to this Cope-Con?"

I said I was.

"Well," Brent said, "there's our project to consider."

"It's true," Nina said, "that no one can re-write history the way you two can."

"How do you know?" I asked.

The old texts were burned as soon as they became obsolete. Sometimes right on publication date. No one could compare the old and new.

"You've always said so," she replied.

"I didn't mean *that* project," Brent said. "I meant the other one." That would be our truth project. It was only a hobby. And something of a joke, like grown men playing hop-scotch and heatedly defending its utility. We were trying to put together an un-Anny history of the last eight decades.

I shrugged.

Brent said he had to go. "Good luck. If I don't see you again, it's been fun." He went.

The kid from down-hall came through the door.

"Ma wants to know if she can borrow the salt."

"No," I said. "We ate it all."

We were finally alone.

The 106th level of League Residence Manor 72 showed us a panoramic view of convoluted, interlocking buildings. Down below, small islands of concrete separated one complex from another. In the distance other Anny manors were distinguishable: Blues, Greens, Browns, Yellows . . .

I got up and approached the tell-viewer, removed the soft board from the oval's rear, and sticking in a hasty hand, checked the hidden scrambler—it was becoming a mania with me. It was fine, which meant we were still safe from bugging. I returned the pliable board to its customary position, and said:

"There's your reason, if you still want one. That's why I'm going."

The girl pulled a face and shook her head. "That's not what I meant." Cool gray-green eyes gazed out at me from a cream-colored complexion; full lips were bent in a slight pout. Blonde, almost sandy hair hung waist length. She was quite beautiful. And naked.

Also bereft of clothing, I padded back to the bed, slipped under the cool sheets. I said, "Come on."

The girl, lifting her end of the sheet, wiggled under.

We lay there not touching, both staring up at the ceiling. Presently, I turned on an elbow. "It's like this," I said. "Someone's got to save us from ourselves, and I'm one of the glinks who's going to do it."

"If you must be a heretic, Jimmy," she said, "why can't it be poetry or history?"

"Poetry?"

"They don't shoot you for that."

"Why should they?"

"And you like poetry. I saw you reading one once, right?"

"I love the stuff. And I did read one once. It's a sanctioned heresy, after all. Who needs it? Getting caught with those history glinks is something else: it's the stockade. I'd personally rather be shot. Anyway, what can those historians do? Print up a clandestine think-text? Look, ever hear of Marx? Einstein? Russell? Idea men. Expunged now, of course, but once pretty damned potent. To carry out their ideas, however, organizations were needed. Big, stormy ones—not unlike the Copernicans."

The Copes were an underground network of scientists recruited from all Annys. Their aim was to topple the retrogressive Anny structure and replace it with an open society. I was one of them.

"The Copes are just scientists, that's all," Nina complained.

"Not just. Why do you say just? They *do* things, in the real world; they make things happen."

"All right, since when are *you* a scientist?"

"Me? Who said I was a scientist? I'm a minor executive, honey; I make some of the wheels turn."

"The Copes," she said, "can do quite nicely without you, this once. There's going to be trouble at their convention, Jimmy."

"Says who?"

"Gabler."

"The clerk?"

"He should know, shouldn't he?"

"On good days he can even tell where the bureau's at, if he's lucky."

"And Ronda?"

"Newman?"

"Ronda Newman, Neels' under-sec." Neels was a big wheel in the League set-up.

"What does Neels know?"

"You'll see. They'll cart you all away—far, far away. And then they'll shoot you."

I had a rejoinder for that one. "They'd have done it long ago—if they could."

"I love you," she said. "And I don't want anything bad to happen. Ever."

"It won't, don't worry; they've got to find us first. They haven't yet. Why should they now?"

"I'm going to worry all the same."

"Come here."

"No."

I put out my hand.

"Oh," she said.

"I'll come back," I said, "because of this."

"Oh!" she said.

Mangus came in.

"Excuse me," he said.

"No," I said.

"It's a pear or apple I be needing," he said.

"Clear out," I said.

Mangus left.

"I love you," I said. "You like this?"

"Yes-s. You *know* I do. I love that."

"How much?"

"Oh, *so* much."

"Yes?"

"You know I do. Oh!"

"Very, very much?"

"Oh, so much; so very much."

"Tell me."

"Yes, I do! I love it. Yes, I do. I do. I do. Don't take your hand away. Jimmy, I love you so much. Oh!"

"I love you too," I said, rolling over to her.

"Yes, Jimmy. Oh God."

"Darling."

"Oh, that's so good."

"It always is. Always. Because of you."

"It's got to be."

"Yes."

"Brother and sister."

"Yes."

"Because we're brother and sister."

"My darling, for always, for always."

"It's better with brother and sister. Right? Right? Isn't it, Jimmy. Isn't it?"

"It's got to be. You know it. Brother and sister love."

"Oh, Jimmy."

"Yes!"

"Oh, now! Come here to sister. Come here now. Oh. Now, now. Oh God, yes."

Down the long corridor a shimmering sign spelled out:

LEAGUE

And below that, in smaller letters:

SUB-GROUP

And below that:

INCEST CULT

That was then.

Now I was in between the trees. Sunlight came through the leaves, through webs of twining, climbing vines like some organic grille-work.

I pictured country roads of long ago with pastures, farm houses, sheep grazing, cattle, whatever they had in those days. Who could tell? Buffalo, perhaps. There'd be chickens, of course. Corn. Wheat. Barley. All under the sun.

They'll find you, a voice inside me seemed to whisper. As if a part of my mind had grown malicious and mean-spirited, had turned against the other, more hopeful part. If you're very unlucky, it won't be ransomers (for they wait by the city speedway and you are nowhere near there), it won't be slavers (although it could be), it won't even be revengers (who'd stab quickly, mercifully, when deciding against you), but others . . .

Ransomers would contact the League. It would simply mean exchanging one dying for another, like a man burning at the stake asking to be drowned instead. Slavers meant a long, protracted, living death. And revengers might—but probably would not—make me one of them. There'd be the months or even years of probation, of steely-eyed surveillance—like a monkey on a long-chain—of semi-servitude and the constant hunt for new victims. That was their only goal. Revengers were almost all illiterate, their career graphs hovering in the fives and tens. And that'd work against me, coming as I did from another echelon. No, they wouldn't want me; in the end I'd be poor material . . .

But here others predominated, were, in fact, the vast majority. If I met anyone, it'd be:

Sloots.

I knew panic wouldn't help, and quite possibly neither would anything else. I'd try to keep awake, keep alert. That was all I could do.

A muddy clearing. I waded through, working my way laboriously up a small grassy knoll, then plunged back down among the trees, running and tripping, stepping over six-foot hunks of rusted drain pipe, plowing through thick underbrush and foliage, till I came to another clearing, heaving aside a cluster of branches . . .

This other clearing stopped me cold.

I stared. Blinked. Looked again.

I had plain forgotten; somehow it had slipped my mind, as if my memories had begun to sweat out of my pores as I ran.

Of course it was here: the outpost. I'd even seen its interior once —years ago, on a quick field trip run by League historians. The Alliance had stood us to lunch; who could forget a thing like that?

My eyes now traveled the length of the building.

Three stories of solid metal.

Box-like. Impregnable. The towering fence an ever-ready, watchful guardian. It was all there.

An Alliance Outpost.

Isolated.

Buried.

Where none should be.

A lighthouse in the wilderness. Which was lightless. Useless. As though a prankster had chosen this spot to erect a monument to futility.

A decade earlier there'd been talk of a project, all right, an Alliance safety-way to the city: new manors and produce marts—a complete mini-center. The League—in those days—had weighed a similar move, had hopes of backing up the jungle. *The blight* came instead. But the outpost remained.

No signs of life now. Soundless. Motionless. Shuttered windows. A think-text diagram of an outpost in hostile terrain. Sunlight caught the wire fence, sent dancing beams off the thick electric coils. But unlike the Association, this Anny had a League hook-up: call-boxes connected the two Annys.

That made it worthwhile.

I walked to the fence and at once heard it say:

"*Request medallion*." The voice sounded squeaky, like metal bedsprings. Hair on the back of my neck started to rise. Fumbling in my pocket, I produced the medallion—thank goodness for that medallion—a two-inch copper coin bearing the League imprimatur and my thumb print. An instant to scan. The fence boomed, "*Medallion acknowledged*," and I put the coin away. The fence was talking as if my presence certified its humanity, made us equals. "*All acts of an aggressive nature are proscribed; a force beam, directed by the computer eye, is centered on you to insure compliance with all lawful Alliance regulations. It will remain so for the duration of your stay. Acknowledge.*"

I did, as sudden hysteria bubbled inside me. I bit my lip, resisted the impulse to somehow *taunt* the fence. A madman's urge. And only a madman would be out here in the first place. But if I appeared deranged, the doctrine of *Safe Conduct* wouldn't hold. My prospects would be the stockade, another stroke on the H graph.

Something clicked and part of the fence swung in.

Stepping through, I saw a thin, sour-looking man of medium height, considerably older than myself, waiting motionless in the now-open outpost doorway. A maroon robe covered green pajamas; hair was gray, face long, narrow, and unshaven. He watched me approach with unconcealed amazement, suspicion distorting his features, as if one of the trees had walked up to ask for a handout. But surely he wasn't worried. Merely annoyed; curious perhaps.

Ransomer?

Slaver?

Revenger?

Sloot?

Madman?

The computer would see to it, could handle it all.

Heretic?

The computer would check.

"Well, sir?" the old man spoke curtly.

Only a short while after sunrise. In the jungle there'd be no need to rise early; I'd roused this oldster from his bed.

I said, "Call-box," and was thankful that etiquette required no more. *Neither could this keep ask.*

He's searching his mind now, I knew, trying to dredge up a question, a probe. As though he were thumbing a procedure-text, page by page, inside his skull. It won't help. What can he say to a Leaguer, an anny from another *Anschluss?* The computer would scan and check . . . but if I'm in *good standing,* I must remain an enigma . . . and with luck my number hadn't quite come up yet.

At the word "call-box" the man nodded, stepped aside. *Ritual.*

The first chamber was an almost-bare, green-walled waiting room. A call-box hung from the west wall. Nothing else. Trust the Alliance, here you spoke standing up. At attention. I didn't mind. I'd have spoken upside down just to get at that box.

I went toward it now, slowly, my back to the other man.

No alarm.

No force beam.

There was nothing.

And by this time the computer must have checked.

Still a League anny, after all. *In good standing.*

At least as far as the H check was concerned.

I was breathing again.

But they needn't have bothered with the H check. Sooner or later the League itself would catch up with me. Food marts. Manors. I'd have to stop at one of them. Posted? There'd be more important fish to fry. I could wait my turn. After all—where would I go? Where, indeed?

"That's all you want?" the keep's voice came from behind me. "The call-box?"

"That's it."

I dialed the controller.

"Yes-s?" a distant voice.

"League 7-9029X," I said.

"One moment please-ss."

I waited.

Behind me, the keep cleared his throat.

The controller said, "I'm *sor'rry.* All League lines are *bus-sy.*"

"I'll tell you," the keep said.

"I'll wait," I told the call-box.

"Very *well-ll*."

"You know Willgear," the keep was beginning.

"Deposit controller fee *please*."

I dropped the coins into the slot.

"Thank you-u-u."

"Willgear, now," the keep said, "there was a Lacer, wasn't he?"

Willgear, the think-text. Well, there was really no way around it. Everything has its price. This was cheap, dirt cheap.

"Now that's true, ain't it?" the keep's voice was rising, insistent.

"A very wise man," I said.

"None better," the keep shouted.

"Controller," I said, pressing the stud.

"Yes-ss?"

"Martin Braitwood Willgear!" the keep shouted triumphantly.

I said, "Could you try that League number again, please?"

"One mo-*ment*, please."

"Listen, you," the keep said. "You see this?"

I glanced over my shoulder. The keep was only waving a small green book.

"Here's knowledge!" the keep yelled.

"I am sorry," the controller said, "the lines are still *bus-sy*."

I licked dry lips. This call-box system had never worked, but lately it'd really started going to pieces.

"He knows a thing," the keep was shouting, waving his book, "wouldn't you say? He's got an answer or two, huh? He don't go in for no smart-aleck slickery like some . . ."

No, he doesn't, I thought; the people who put Willgear together had absolutely no sense of humor. But Willgear had to be a giant step ahead of Swain. The Federation's Swain was nothing more than a raving psychotic. Almost as if there actually *had* been a Swain— some mental defective spewing out his nightmare imaginings— rather than a shrewd, willful committee.

"Discipline!" the keep was hollering. "You got to stand the think."

I kept nodding. Here he is, the new man, tomorrow's Everyman. No, it didn't really matter how you put the Annys together. The end product would be this.

The keep was saying, "Martin Braitwood Willgear, yes sir, he could *teach* you Leaguers . . ."

I heard myself agreeing.

The keep paced back and forth: "Know how? Know how?"

I said that there must be lots of ways.

"You said it, you said it."

The controller: "Do you still wish to wait, *sir-rr*?"

"Can't you put it through yet, controller?"

"The lines are *still-ll* busy."

"I'll tell you the ways," the keep said. "You listenin'?"

"Of course." How could I help it?

The keep said, "He'd show you the truth; you Leaguers wouldn't be Leaguers no more. Know what you'd be?"

I thought a very vile word.

"Alliancers! That's what," the keep screamed.

I realized my word wasn't vile enough and pasted a smile on my face like an idiot's mask.

"A giant mind!" the keep screamed, as though reaffirmation of the sage must lend stature to the disciple. "Saw how cooks got to work with electricians, 'cause there ain't no other way; saw how drummers needed the woodsmith's hand; saw how it all come together, was good, was right; yes sir, he *knew!* He took the real estate man, mind you, and tied him to the soft-drink maker; made us all a team, he did—sacrifice and discipline. It took vision. It took planning. Martin Braitwood Willgear did that. Did the man-thing. Didn't rush none. Took the sign painters, put 'em in with the clean-up crews. That took some doing. That took some foresight. 'Cause they didn't want to be together; didn't see the wisdom of it. But the wisdom was there, just needed bringing out, was all, needed a *man* to show 'em . . ."

Great God, he's got it memorized, right from the think-text.

"You may go ahead *now-ww*," the controller said. "There is a two-index toll charge."

I fed the box its ransom, held up a hand for the outposter, hoping etiquette would seal his lips. There was sudden quiet behind me. A tip of the old Norton hat to decorum.

Ringing. A click. "There is no one here at this time. When the message ends, you will have sixty seconds to leave name, Anny, and number. Thank you."

The voice was mine. As if days before I had consciously laid a trap to mock my later self.

Well, so much for that. *Only where could she be?* Early morning. Nina ought to have been home. I could still leave a message of some kind; but if there'd been trouble, if I'd been League-posted, they might have tagged my call-box with a tracer. A message wasn't worth it.

I put down the receiver.

Brent? In all probability, Brent—the perennial lady's man—wouldn't be at his *official* residence. The call-box no longer seemed so good an idea. It rang.

Behind me the keep's voice: "For you, anny."

I lifted the receiver.

"That will be one index disconnect fee."

The call-box swallowed another index.

"*Thank you-ww.*"

"More?" the keep asked ritualistically.

"No."

"Hang on, anny."

The keep went away, came back an instant later.

I took the small package he offered, knowing what it must contain. I nodded once and left the building almost at a trot. I was glad to go. The fence clicked open, clicked shut behind me.

I hurled away the little green book as if it were some unclean object, a source of instant contamination, and started hiking.

The jungle was back.

And something else.

Loping.
Scrambling.
Chattering.
Screeching.

Over bushes, tree trunks, mounds of earth, outcroppings of rock. They came.

Barefoot.

Tattered.

Emaciated.

Ribs jutting, cheekbones hollow, hunger distorting their faces.

Sloots!

How many?

Twenty? Thirty? A hundred?

I couldn't tell.

They came from all sides now, rising out of the thicket, reaching, groping, stumbling. Almost as if the zoo had flung open its ape-house doors.

I turned and ran.

Before me, a woman sprang up; my fist met her in a looping arch; she fell down; I ran over her. Men ran after me—yelping, cursing men. One fell on me from a tree, bringing me to my knees; he twined long, bony arms around my neck; he squeezed. I twisted around and put a finger in his right eye. Screaming, he let go. I was up and running. Three of them ahead. I turned right. Two of them. I dodged behind one tree, another, doubled over now so they couldn't see me. I heard their screaming, their rage, and knew they wouldn't give it up; knew their cries would bring others. Reach the Alliance outpost again? Backtrack? I saw them—nine of them—blocking my way, and knew that the outpost was sealed off. I turned away; it's done, over, I thought. I wondered if I could strip, pull off my clothes, become one of them? And knew I couldn't: too much fat on me; my hair too short, too clean; I had no beard. I thought, Yes, even here among these things a social order still exists, still governs, so that outsiders made the best prey. Fortunate things, to have hit on the one strategy that might preserve their wretched lives. My feet flew over tangled earth; bright multi-colored leaves sparkled in the sun; shadows dappled my path; roots, twigs, soft mud, and dugouts tripped and turned me. I couldn't breathe, couldn't see, couldn't hear. Their yells, my breathing, our running flooded together in one piercing scream.

I stumbled, hands gripped me, three sloots clung to me like tar paper. I heard their hissing breath, smelled their stinking bodies; beyond them I sensed the coming of others.

I thought, What can you expect, after all, from minus-five career graphs?

And then I thought nothing at all. I went blank like a used-up light bulb. I shorted out.

FLEISHER TWO

THE TOOL-WORKS

The guard waved them through the gate, only glancing at Eddy Fleisher's pass.

The gate swung shut behind them.

Eddy Fleisher put his foot on the accelerator.

Fence, gate and guard-post receded behind them, sank into the darkness. Fog rolled over the grounds. Gravel churned under wheels. The Studebaker cut through the night, its headlights cleaving the blackness. Not unlike a butcher slicing through a tenderloin, Fleisher thought. But then, not quite like that either.

Beside him, Tom Lacy said:

"Let's drop it, huh?" He had been saying it often and loudly, his face an oblong patch in the dimness, his voice watery.

Fleisher said:

"Shut up."

"Aw, Eddy."

"It's in the bag," Eddy Fleisher told him. "Stop beefing. We get Earl off the hook—we hit the jackpot. What's so tough about that?"

"Doin' it."

"You're a sorehead, Tom. Stop it. Want to stay a pork-and-beaner all your days?"

"You givin' me a choice?"

"No."

"Honest to God, Eddy, if I'd known you was gonna pull a stunt like this, I wouldn't of braced you—"

Fleisher put a sneer in his voice. "Yellow?" he asked.

"Damn right."

"Do me a favor, Tom."

"What's that, Eddy?"

"Shut up."

"Aw, Jesus, Eddy . . ."

A short wooden bridge bounced under them. The road turned to tar. Up ahead the plant loomed. Night covered it; fog swept over it. Light shimmered from two windows high up near the roof of the first building, spread to a twinkling smear on the waves of fog.

They whisked on by.

Other buildings followed. They went by them too. After a while Eddy Fleisher doused the headlights, cut their speed, creeping along now past one structure, then another. Fleisher lowered a window. Damp fog floated in. Car wheels made muffled sounds on the roadway; the engine purred softly. Tar had turned to concrete now. There were no other sounds. No lights. A moment passed; Eddy Fleisher saw what he had come to see, killed the engine, stopped. In the silence that followed, Fleisher half-turned to his companion, nodded once. "We're here," he said, was answered by a grunt.

A huge, many-faceted plant stretched before them, brick and concrete. One of the main ones. As neat, elegant, and homey a package as any Hooverville you ever saw, Fleisher reflected, only built more solid, made to last, so it could bring in the green. Not the worst place to spend a lifetime. But close, too close.

Factory 6B. The early morning hours, wispy fog, and quiet made it seem a dreamy spot, a slumberland print designed for the kiddies' room. There was nothing in that.

The assembly line wasn't their destination, Fleisher told his accomplice; they'd avoid the metal works and pipe lines. The top floors held the quarry.

Eddy Fleisher pushed open the car door, got out.

From the trunk, he removed a leather satchel, handed it to Lacy. "You carry this," he said.

"What's this?"

"The gear."

"What gear?"

"Some pineapples."

A sick laugh came from the darkness. "You ribbin' me?"

"What do you think?" Fleisher said.

"Shit, Eddy—"

Fleisher closed the trunk, first stuffing the pockets of his mackinaw with an array of items: tools, guns, a dimmer. A few more bits and pieces and he'd've needed a union card to lug them around, he thought bitterly. This was a cockeyed profession, all right: the hours were flighty as butterflies, but the pay could sometimes be a honey. "I'm kidding," he said to Lacy, "it's really a lounging robe and slippers."

"You said no shootin'." Lacy's voice was reproachful.

"I didn't say that. I said no one'd get shot. Not us, at least. There's a difference, pal."

Wet grass squished underfoot. Lacy plodded behind Fleisher, satchel in tow.

"Watch how you lug that," Fleisher said earnestly.

Lacy said nothing.

Eddy Fleisher, jerking a thumb at the black visor of his gray cap, went down on one knee like an aspiring Al Jolson and peered at the lock of the first door they came to. It was only a lock. Lacy stood by, impatiently shifting from one foot to another like a man waltzing on hot coals. He held the bag delicately with both hands, as if it were a carton of slightly cracked eggs his shrewish missus had warned him to bring home without a loss.

The lock sprang open after a long twisted wire fiddled with it.

The two men went up a steep flight of stone steps; a door on the third-floor landing led them to a darkened hallway which curved around a wall; the pair, following this wall, found another door, also unlocked, and went up wooden stairs. Two flights of this and they reached a fourth door. Fleisher inched it open; behind him he heard Lacy's shallow breathing. Fleisher peered down a longish dark hallway. At its far left fingers of light bent around a corner, spread out on the carpeted floor like puddles of make-believe beverage. No factory stink here. Smells of floor wax, typewriter ribbons, and reams of bonded paper. A classy joint.

Lacy, craning his long neck, stuck his head over Fleisher's right shoulder, squinted down the hall.

"Nothin'!" he announced, as though he liked the idea.

"Uh-uh. They're there, all right."

"Guess-work," Lacy said contemptuously. "Whaddya gonna do?"

"You'll see."

"Look," he said, grabbing Fleisher's arm. "Shouldn't we maybe scout around like first?"

"No."

Leaving the stairwell's cover, the pair tiptoed up the hall, away from light into the darkness of a side corridor, feeling their way along until presently they reached a closet; in it, brooms, mops, dust pans, spare garbage containers.

A sink was next to the closet.

Over this sink, barely distinguishable—a fuse box. Fleisher put a hand up in the dark. He whispered, "It's a gut," and began removing the fuses.

Soon the juice was off on the entire floor.

Lacy said, "They won't like this."

"Uh-huh. Let's you and me step in the closet."

Elbowing their way in between brooms and mops, they left a minimal slit between door and frame. Stale air smelled of Lysol, dust, and rotting mops.

Eddy Fleisher and Tom Lacy waited.

Soon feet were heard. A light suddenly lit their door, moved on. One pair of feet.

Fleisher took a gun from his pocket. Pausing for a deep breath, he shoved open the door.

A man's back was to him; one shirt-sleeved hand groped for the fuse box, the other held a dimmer. It was a posture Eddy Fleisher could approve of.

"They're not there," he said. "I took them out."

The man's body jerked as he wheeled, surprise on his flabby face. His trousers, Fleisher saw, were blue with a black stripe down the side: part of a guard's uniform.

He said evenly:

"Better freeze, brother."

The guard showed poor sense. A fanatic.

His right hand dived for a pocket, a bulging one. Fleisher could guess what it held.

He stabbed out with his gun, caught the guard on the head, hit him again, making a soft dull sound like a pitched apple hitting a brick wall. The guard fell down, dropping his dimmer; it rolled around on the floor.

The guard—still not satisfied—looked as though he might want to scramble up on wobbly hands and knees and continue the bout.

Eddy Fleisher told him:

"Don't do it, mister."

The guard was still paying no attention to Fleisher. Fleisher didn't like that. Fleisher raised his foot and kicked him in the mouth.

The guard's eyes went wide with newly-acquired knowledge, his chin colliding with the floor. Blood began to trickle through his lips. He groaned once and didn't move.

"That's good," Eddy Fleisher encouraged this right thinking. Here was a man he might get along with.

Tom Lacy picked up the dimmer, played it around.

"Upsy-daisy," Fleisher said.

Lacy took away the guard's gun.

"See this?" Eddy Fleisher said, showing him *his* gun.

The ghee looked at Eddy Fleisher, looked at the gun, looked at Tom Lacy. Blinking, he said, "What is this?" He was a smart one all right, but probably not quite Einstein; Fleisher answered accordingly:

"How many others with you?"

The guard screwed up his eyes at Fleisher. "You guys reds?" he said.

Lacy said, "Let's shoot him."

The guard wiped blood from his lips. "Two."

"See, Lacy? Only two." To the guard Fleisher said, "You got Earl Kneely."

"We got him."

"Had him," Lacy said.

A dull light seemed to flicker in the guard's puffy eyes. He said slowly:

"You with Kneely, eh?"

"Earl's with us," Lacy said. There was pride in his voice.

"I figured you was reds," the man said. "You're just punks."

"Let's shoot him," Lacy said.

"He doesn't want that," Fleisher said; to the guard he said, "Do you?"

The guard said he didn't.

"That's the ticket," Eddy Fleisher said. "Now we go back to your pals. No one gets hurt. All you gotta do is pay attention to what I say, do what I tell you. You got that?" It seemed simple enough, even redundant.

The guard nodded.

Eddy Fleisher said:

"When the lights blew, you birds figured what?"

"A fuse."

"What're you using for light now?"

The guards had a couple of flashes set up.

"Let's walk," Eddy Fleisher said.

The trio went up the hall.

"When I say now," Fleisher explained, "you sing out to your pals, 'I can't fix it.' Make sure you do it right. You don't want trouble."

"No," he said. "Who wants trouble?"

"You've got the right attitude."

"You're still punks."

"Times are tough."

"You've got a point, brother," he said.

Faint light presently warned Fleisher he was approaching his target; he put his gun in the guard's back, whispered, "Now."

The guard called out:

"I can't fix it."

A voice called back:

"Why not?" The voice didn't sound as though it meant it.

Fleisher, Lacy, and the guard trooped into a white-walled room. Another guard—a tall one—lay on an iron cot; a third—equally tall, but thinner—sat at a bare wooden table whose right front leg was missing an inch; a book propped it up, the mark of refinement. This third man fingered a deck of cards. He did nothing else.

Weak light spread from three dimmers strategically placed on a table.

The pair looked at their visitors.

The visitors showed them their guns. "Don't be heroes," Fleisher spoke up.

"Not me," the man on the cot promised immediately.

The one at the table raised his empty hands over his head. "See?" he said. "I'm docile."

"Stand up," Fleisher told them.

They did, in a hurry.

"Rope," Fleisher said.

All three guards pointed to a green tin cabinet over in a corner, wagged their heads in unison. They'd've done great in a chorus line.

"Tom."

Lacy found the rope.

"Who are you gents?" the guy with the hoisted hands inquired politely.

"Doc Savage," Fleisher explained.

The guards were faced toward the wall.

Lacy bound them. Eddy Fleisher called:

"Earl!"

A muffled voice answered through a locked door.

"Key," Eddy Fleisher said, still scotch with the syllables.

"Table drawer," one of the trio responded.

"Thanks, pal."

"Don't mention it. You aim to leave us like this?"

"They'll find you in the morning."

"Have a heart, Mac."

"You think this is a picnic?" Eddy Fleisher asked using the key on the door. Over Fleisher's shoulder Tom Lacy said, "'Lo, Earl."

Earl Kneely stepped through. The floor creaked only a little bit but didn't give way. It was just luck. He was bigger than Fleisher, bigger than Lacy. His legs like tree trunks, his belly a collection of beer barrels. A round head resembling a beach ball, but not as pretty. Only two chins; they were enough. A nose that was just that —only larger. Bloated lips. Heavy eyelids. Straight black hair pasted back over an expanse of wide skull.

This was the man Eddy Fleisher had come to rescue. It didn't quite make him the Scarlet Pimpernel.

"Who's this?" Earl Kneely asked meaningfully, his voice a hoarse squeak.

"Your benefactor," Eddy Fleisher said.

"Our fence," Tom Lacy said. Fleisher didn't blush. He'd been called worse things with just as much truth in them.

Earl Kneely looked down at Fleisher, studied his face, mackinaw, peaked cap, two-toned shoes. After considering these items carefully, he held out a beefy paw.

"I'm tickled," he said simply.

They shook on that.

"Enough shooting the breeze," Eddy Fleisher complained.

His two companions ducked their heads over this statement. It was irrefutable.

The trio trotted for the hall.

The guards, trussed up, sat facing the wall—in poses that, at first glance, spoke of deep meditation.

Gold lettering on the office door read:

KRAFT PROTECTION AGENCY

Fleisher had to admit they'd done a swell job on this Earl Kneely. There seemed to be nothing missing from what must have been his three hundred pounds. But then Fleisher didn't know what he'd looked like before. King Kong, maybe.

So far it was all going by the book. He'd suckered Tom, sprung Earl, and they were all making their back-door sneak together. One happy family. Not bad—considering he was the Joe who'd blown the whistle on Kneely in the first place.

NORTON THREE

THE TUNNEL

Somehow I was alone.
  Still in the woods.
  My hands were covered with blood. It wasn't mine.
  I could still hear sloots, somewhere behind me.
  My clothing was torn, blood-spattered. No pain, others' blood.
  What had happened? How had I managed to cut loose from a herd of sloots? *And why couldn't I remember?*
  My eyes shifted in and out of focus, the scene before me hazing over as if mist were rolling over the forest, then springing into pinpoint relief as though a high-powered telescope were being manipulated.
  Noises swelled—hunger-crazed, maddened sloots growing closer again. A symphony of the damned.
  Run. Run. Run.

  The mound of earth was taller than a man.
  Dead leaves.
  Dried bark.
  Branches.
  Without preamble I began to dig.
  I used both hands, working swiftly, panic nipping at every motion.
  A compost heap, I thought, that's all it is. *What am I doing?*
  I dug on.
  The ground seemed to tremble.
  I dug some more.

There was a sound directly beneath my feet.

I glanced down, stupidly. I might still have jumped aside. I didn't.

The ground opened up under me.

I went down.

Plunging.

Earth spilled after me, cascaded over me, filled my eyes, ears, and mouth. A deluge of earth.

The light from above winked out like some giant eyelid closing over.

I lay quite still—the darkness was total—and vaguely wondered what had happened to me.

I didn't hear the sloots above me. If they were up there, I guessed I would probably not be able to hear them; I'd fallen too far. Trying to move, I found that I could. Nothing seemed broken. Luck of a kind, at least. *But where the hell was I?* Slowly I freed myself from the pile of earth and got to my feet.

Still darkness.

Pitch black overhead.

They'd never find me here. No one would.

The dirt began to itch.

A deep hole. Someone had dug a hole in the jungle. And I had found it and fallen in.

Only how deep? How far down did it go? *And why?*

Was I on a ledge, some kind of scaffold? Was I about to step off into nothing?

Don't move! Don't move! Don't move!

Hysteria capered in me; I wanted to scream, to bellow at the top of my lungs. I could sympathize now with the claustrophobic. I had become their blood brother.

The air was incredibly stale, torture to breathe. Layers on layers of dust. Generations of decay and disuse. Or was it?

I'd never get out!

Scream and the things would find me; scream and the sloots would come and dig me out. Then nothing would matter. Because there could be no one here to help me. Only sloots—and sloots weren't human. Not quite.

But they had been once.

I'd assumed the outposter, the true believer, to be the final and absolute goal of the Annys—as the Annys, no doubt, had themselves assumed.

We were both wrong.

The outposter was, after all, merely another rung on the ladder. No sooner in ascendency than obsolete, an anachronism, as used-up as last year's think-tape. At best, only a fleeting instant in history, an eye-blink.

They had forgotten the sloots.

Chairman Lancaster had erred.

The tall, thin leader with the line mustache, bony face, and nervous gestures had spoken passionately in his last bi-monthly think-talk. The hall, as usual, was packed with middle- and upper-echelon League historians routed out especially for the occasion. On stage, the cherubic, rotund figure of Father Pen was seated to the right of the dais. To the left, Joe Dermus, baldheaded, stooped; Philip Brandon, wide and confident; Stephen Neels, prim as always; and Farber Millard, blond and relaxed, rounded out the assembled League Lacers.

Chairman Lancaster spoke of the Proto-Annys that day. Of the hazy, forgotten nineteen-thirties and their special heroes. Father Coughlin, a rabble-rouser who had built, through his fiery radio harangues, a dedicated, unswerving, Anny-like following.

Dr. Francis E. Townsend, who had come up with The Townsend Old-Age Revolving Pensions Plan, calling for a $200-a-month allowance for every citizen over sixty, and had splendidly won the allegiance of a goodly segment of aged.

The Share Our Wealth Program of Senator "Kingfish" Huey Long, still another glittering triumph of Anny-like think-texts.

And before that, of course, there had been the Technocracy craze . . .

Lancaster had concluded in his high, scratchy voice, stressing his moral, that substance played no role in belief. Any think-text would do. If emotively applied and socially reinforced, it would stick.

After the think-talk I made my way to the Chairman's side. What

I asked had bordered on heresy: "Is it true, sir, that the history vaults are . . . abridged?"

Dell Lancaster had turned his bony face in my direction and produced a tired smile. Historians were granted a certain latitude.

"What does it matter?" he asked simply.

"Facts—" I began.

"You weren't listening," Lancaster cut me short.

Father Pen put his arm around my shoulder, large eyes twinkling in a round face. "Jimmy here is one of our Incests—up and coming, a very bright lad."

The Chairman nodded good-naturedly. "Any facts will do, Jimmy. Annys are permanent. Facts come and go."

"And faithful annys," Neels added, "go on forever."

"Do they now?" Pen said.

Lancaster was emphatic. "It's beyond question!"

Dermus, Brandon, and Millard nodded their agreement.

But they had been wrong wrong wrong.

The annys would never inherit the earth.

But something else might.

Take an anny, train him for one job, one slot, one way of life, and that'll be all he knows. Similarly, League tell-viewers were only good for League tape-outs: one channel. Just like the other Annys. Learn in the Anny think-rooms and you learn what the Annys want.

But trade often brought annys together. There were treaties, pacts, understandings between the Annys. No Anny was self-sufficient. And glinks got to look at competing channels after all . . .

Some might wonder . . . might become *confused* . . .

The treaties broke down; pledges went for naught; the Annys splintered and rotted. There was turmoil—

No food.

No clothing.

No gas one day, no water the next.

The age of the NOs.

The time of the *second blight.*

Only the NOs wouldn't admit it.

We'll all go down together.
Bloodbaths.
Killings.
Riots.
Work with your mind and you'd be fair game for a hundred heresies. A seeming way out, something to believe in. But a manual knew nothing. When you caught a heretic, you shot him. Or locked him in the stockade for a decade or two. But when a mani stepped out of line, he was simply given the gate, along with his brood. *Gated out* to starve in the jungle. The other Annys wouldn't touch him. And the heresies were too weak, too poor, too frightened, or too *Lacer* to lend a hand.

You were a mani.
You knew nothing to begin with and you knew less now.
You starved.
And day by day you became less human.
You might become—revenger, slaver, ransomer.
But more likely you merely became a sloot.
Lord help us all, I thought. In the last days of the second blight, in the time of the twilight hours, all men shall become *things* . . .

The darkness pressed in on me. I didn't lose my head; I couldn't afford to panic now. Slowly I sank to my knees, put out my hands and touched earth. I began to crawl, inch by inch. I found concrete. Cracked. Chipped. Broken. I ran my fingers over it again. Amazed! Concrete under the jungle. I heard only my own breathing, only my own movements and the shifting of earth and debris under me. I saw nothing.

Blind?

Had I gone blind? Perhaps the fall had affected my vision?

I felt the tons of earth on all sides of me. Crushing earth. Killing earth. As though earth had taken—for ever and ever—the place of air and sky.

Buried alive!

I sat quite still on the uneven jagged slabs of concrete and told myself a story. It was a simple one.

In this story, I, James Norton, pursued by devils, had had the good sense to let my unconscious assume total control. The *historian* James Norton had known that a city had once stood here. He had studied this city and knew its dimensions. Maps and blueprints of this city—which had, in fact, been a *real* city and not a concoction of mere dogma—had remained in his mind, somewhere on a sub-level, perhaps, but there nonetheless, waiting to be summoned on demand.

I'd fallen through into some hole that I had known, all along, would be there.

I was certainly not buried alive.

Nor blind.

With any luck I'd be able to crawl out, soon find a way up the dug-out wall. I'd wait until the sloots departed, as they surely must after a time, and then continue on my way.

There was nothing to be afraid of.

Panic was my only enemy.

If I kept my head, I'd be all right.

From further inside the tunnel a very small, reedy voice said, "Come, come now, my dear fellow, don't just *sit* there, do pick me up . . ."

I stared into the darkness, riveted, muscles taut.

The voice came again: "Oh dear."

I shrieked, "WHO'S THERE?!" My nerves were as jumbled as a nod-hooker's dreams.

"Yes," the voice said, "one moment . . ."

I did what I could, gathered my legs under me, summoned my failing resources, readied myself for the attack that would surely come. I would die. That was quite clear now. I would do so, however, with dignity. Actually, I'd have preferred clawing my way up the wall, only I didn't know how . . .

"My dear Norton," the voice said.

So they had my name, too. How the hell had they managed that? What kind of idiotic trap was this? A scheme to break me? To make me implicate the others? It was senseless. Un-Leaguish. Who went in for entrapments these days? Not the Annys. They had better, surer methods. Anyway, my fellow Copers were probably dead ducks by now. The League would have all the answers it needed for the asking.

Still there was no attack.

Perhaps the fall had done something to my mind?

I called out, "What do you want?" It didn't come out with quite the force and determination I'd intended, but at least I'd gotten the words past my larynx. That would show them I meant business.

If they were really there.

Probably they weren't.

But would that be an improvement?

"Why, my dear Norton," the voice spoke, "to help you. What else?"

I could think of a number of what-elses, all equally distressing.

"Make a light," I said.

Now I'd see a thing or two—if there was anything to see, that is.

"Actually," the voice responded, "I can't . . . at this precise time . . ."

Oh-oh.

The voice went on. "This is most awkward," it said.

You're telling me, I thought; it must be my mind after all; something terrible has happened to it.

But if they'd meant to jump me, they'd have done so by now . . . wouldn't they?

"I am," the voice explained, "slightly *disembodied*; you see?"

I didn't and said so.

"Well," the voice continued testily, "that *is* the situation, my dear fellow. Disembodied. You can therefore imagine the difficulty in granting your simple request . . . which, I might add, appears perfectly justifiable to me . . . under the circumstances. You see?"

Again I didn't.

"Well," the voice said, a note of rising irritability in its tone, "soon there will be a . . . brief moment of illumination . . . a spurt, so to speak . . . soon . . ." The voice trailed off, indecisively.

I could tell the runaround when I was being given the runaround, and said (with more vigor than I felt and less belief in the outcome than I might wish), "What is this?" It was not a memorable question. I was as confused as a tadpole born in a bathtub.

"I," the voice replied, "am a *bubble*."

Well, there it was—the clincher. I was in even bigger trouble than I'd thought.

"Now you know," the bubble said, "and we can get on with the business of saving you."

"I wouldn't mind," I told the blackness truthfully. My echo repeated the statement, as though it made sense. "I'd feel better," I confided, "if you'd tell me a thing or two." I had no real hope.

"Yes?" It sounded eager enough.

"Who are you? How do you know my name? What do you want?"

"M-m-m," the voice said. "Those are *three* things. I have already replied to the latter: to save you. What could be simpler? The preceding queries, I fear, for the moment at least, must remain unanswered. It doesn't really matter, does it, since I am, after all, about to save you?"

"It matters," I said, "to me."

"Unsatisfactory," said the bubble. "You, my dear Norton, are being pig-headed."

It was time I did something. Anything. Only *what*? Quite probably I was insane. In that case, this conversation was with myself. However, the so-called bubble's part of the dialogue was hardly up to my usual high standards of invention. Nevertheless it seemed logical to pursue this odd manifestation of my psyche.

"All right," I said, "so save me; go ahead. I'm all set. I'm ready for it. I'm willing to be saved."

"Bravo," the voice called out to faint sounds of applause. The whole thing was beginning to annoy me. But the feeling, at least, was a definite improvement over raw terror.

"Well?" I said.

"First," the bubble said, "you should know that your error was a grave one."

"Which one?" There'd been lots of them, as I remembered.

"You were returning," the bubble said accusingly, "to the city."

"So?"

"Impossible. You've been posted, Norton. You must turn away

from the city. Absolutely. That is why I chose this moment to inter-
cede—to materialize, as it were. To save you from this danger."

"Well, that's generous—"

"There is no call for impertinence; my intervention here has been
executed at no small expense. You must realize that, obviously, saving you is a matter of some delicacy; it is certainly not child's play.
One might expect a word of gratitude."

"What do you want me to do?"

"We shall, you and I, head for Lab Twenty-nine."

"Twenty-nine?" I said stupidly.

"Precisely."

"The League knows about Twenty-nine. There was trouble. They
must know all our Labs."

"Not Twenty-nine. Trust me."

"They missed it?"

"It was not, my dear fellow, on the list of clandestine outposts.
The list, you see, ended with Twenty-eight!"

In all the Copes had sported twenty-nine hidden labs—bustling
with activity, plans, projects, employing some of the best scientists
and tech-ers—hunting a weapon that might break the Anny stran-
glehold. But this voice was saying the list stopped at Twenty-eight.

"What," I asked, "is so special about Twenty-nine?"

"All in good time," the bubble promised.

That was hardly enlightening.

"I can't do it," I said.

"Can't what?"

"Go with you."

The bubble sputtered. "You're mad."

"That's what I figure."

"Ah! You don't believe in me!"

"That too. But the truth is, I don't go without Nina. My sister."

"But that's utterly fantastic."

"Or Brent."

"Your brother?"

"Partner."

"You are mad."

"I'm sorry," I said.

"The sloots," the voice said, "wait for you above, while in the city you are hunted."

"I'll take my chances."

"You have no chances. Look here, Norton. Do I have your word that if I guide you to the city, you will then follow my advice? Selfless advice, I might add."

I thought it over.

"I take Nina and Brent."

"Certainly."

"All right," I said. I had nothing to lose.

"We are going to Lab Twenty-nine."

"Anything you say." It was fine with me. I had no idea what to make of all this yet. Play along, that was my best prospect. See what came next. I didn't have long to wait.

The bubble said, "What do you remember about how you came to be here?"

"What kind of nonsense is this?"

"Humor me. Tell me what you recall."

I thought. This had better stop soon; as madness goes, it's getting out of hand.

"The sloots chased me."

"And before?"

"The Alliance outpost. I tried to call."

"And before that?"

"The jungle."

"But you spoke to someone?"

"Yes. An outposter. At its edge. I wanted a ride. But he wouldn't take me. There's no Association standard in the city."

"And before."

"Before?"

"You came over the rise."

"Yes. And I saw the city in the distance."

"You recall the Copernicans' Convention?"

"Of course."

"And the trouble?"

"What about it?"

"You remember the trouble?"

I hesitated, my stomach doing a flip-flop.

"I don't know," I said.

Oh Lord, I thought; something *is* wrong. I can't remember the trouble.

I said, "It's not all that clear." And thought: The man in the black mask. He's trying to find out about Weber. That's it. But I don't know *anything* about Weber. No one did. *Except that Weber had founded the Copes.* "Do you want to know about Weber?"

"No," the voice said. "Tell me about Knox."

"Dr. Knox? A physicist. One of the Cope big-wigs. What about him?"

"He was with you when you fled the Cope-Con."

It was coming back to me.

"That's right," I said.

The voice said, "Do you recall the trouble now?"

"I think so."

"All of it?"

"Perhaps."

"It was a raid."

"Yes, a raid."

"Despite your defenses."

"They got around them."

"My dear Norton, they outwitted your Copes at their own game."

"Whose game? The Annys have been around longer. Anyway, we were warned. A little late, that's all."

"You remember it all now?"

Yes, I thought, I seem to.

"Yes," I said.

"Tell me about the raid," the voice said.

I remembered Crawford screaming, blood streaming from his neck. Grant fell.

The lights went out. They had cut the power lines. More screams.

Neuron charges—their odor rampant in the darkness. Delegates crashed into chairs, tables, each other, searching for a way out, exits, safety tunnels. Chaos and turmoil boiled through the hall. Erlich,

Madden, Knox, and myself somehow fought our way through a side door. We tore down a twisting path, reached the car. Others had started with us. They were gone now.

A repeater gun rattled somewhere. There were sounds of running feet.

The four of us piled in; the car lurched forward, took off in pitch blackness, the road shooting by under its wheels.

Somewhere close—too close—behind us, a dark form seemed to follow.

Dead New Jersey townlets, remote, lightless—long deserted—flashed by like worn cardboard cut-outs.

Erlich, the little chemist, drove. Bearded, rotund Knox, eyeglasses like two black perfect circles, kept twisting his neck, nervously glancing back through the rear windows. In the almost total blackness it was now impossible to distinguish anything. We seemed to have lost our pursuers.

We drove lightless.

Our wheels skidded on gravel—the derelict expressway was left behind. The vehicle seemed to shudder. Knox shouted something; Madden was cursing. A tree loomed up ahead; soft grass was suddenly underneath; the car tilted, slid down an embankment, its motor whining, splashed noisily into shallow water.

Erlich started to scream.

The car slowly turned on its side like a hippo taking a dip.

Seconds later I started to crawl over Madden, inadvertently putting a knee in his stomach. Knox was coughing. Fists pounded on the doors, windows. Hands found the release stud, fingers pressed it; the doors silently slid back.

I helped Madden out through the rear; he was wheezing, trembling, trying to catch his breath.

Cold wind stung me, made me shudder. My clothes were wet; there would be no changing for the time being. We stood a foot deep in water. It was no place to be. We began scrambling up the bank. We seemed to be in a dark, wide field. The wind moaned like a lost band of beggars as it rolled around us. To our right, even darker patches might have been trees, a forest. The earth, where the grass was sparse, had turned to mud. Pockets of water swirled in small pits and muddy cavities. No moon or stars: a sheet of clouds formed a very low ceiling over the dark, empty countryside. The air was thick, heavy, drenched in humidity. Crickets, frogs, mosquitoes chorused together in a midnight songfest. It was going to rain again. My eyes had now grown somewhat accustomed to the darkness. I was shivering and my knees shook badly. Objectively, it was impossible to choose a direction, to make much out of the dark shapes that sank into blackness as they veered off into the distance. The gusting wind tossed and tumbled around us with increasing fury, like some fevered animal.

"I am, praise the Lord, unhurt," Dr. Knox bawled over the wind.

Erlich was screaming: "I could not. I could not help it!"

Knox slapped him. It sounded, in that instant, as the wind subsided, like a twig being snapped.

Erlich began to sob.

"We must not—" Knox shouted. A new gust of wind carried away his words. Knox made a megaphone of his hands. He bellowed, "—remain here!"

"Not my fault," Erlich sobbed.

"Separate!" Knox yelled.

Madden ducked his head in agreement.

"Time is precious," Knox yelled.

Erlich said, "My God, my God, my God."

I said, "Madden?"

"What?" The tall man cocked an ear.

I was going to say. What about Erlich? How can we leave Erlich? But I didn't. "Never mind," I yelled. My heart wasn't in it.

"What?" Madden shouted.

I bobbed my head, waved once, and stepped into the darkness. Alone.

I glanced back an instant later, but the other three were already gone.

I started to trot.

Soon time meant nothing.

I went across fields, over hills, along gravel roads; I waded through marshland, stalked through dead towns, stumbled down main streets whose buildings grinned at me out of the darkness with ravaged, moldering faces.

It began to rain.

A churning, whipping downpour. Wind-lashed. A slanting whirlpool of water.

I ran on.

I hadn't given myself better than even odds. I did not think I could elude them. But I knew I must try. At any instant I expected the flare to burst over the fields, a giant exploding finger pinpointing me. But presently, when no flare appeared, I began to consider the possibility—still remote—that the rain might aid me. A lightning storm could scramble their signals, disrupt their finders. Even *their* gadgets might lose their snap out among the elements.

Lightning flickered. The terrain, trees, bushes seemed to take on split-second human proportions, seemed to reach for me.

Then darkness.

Wind tried to lift me, rain to drown me.

But I was putting distance between myself and the NOs.

I ran into trees, branches, bushes; slipped to my knees on wet ground; fell into large puddles; twisted my ankles in holes, pitfalls, depressions. Wind sang in my ears; rain flailed at me; cold numbed my body.

I found a highway and stuck with it. Instinct guided me. I could only guess the direction. No shelter, pause, or rest. The empty fields could offer no refuge. Once the storm abated, they would be after me. The trackers would take over. The hunters would come. My only chance was to move now in the darkness and confusion, move before they organized a search, questioned their captives, drew up the list of suspects . . .

Two hours before sunrise I reached what had once been the George Washington Bridge. Unused. Rusted. As dated as private opinion.

Lightning turned it silver. I ran down its center. I tripped. I ran on, stumbling over my own feet, which had now become serious obstacles. Thunder beat like a celestial drum roll. My feet kept time through the pools of water. Wind and rain made it a trio.

An automatic trucker picked me up on the other side, near 181st Street. Two union watchers sat in the huge programmed vehicle— one of the last inter-Anny conveyances. They had only two buttons to press, stop and go. I told them where I was headed as the trucker glided down the speedway.

The small watcher whistled.

The husky one wished me good luck.

The trucker was bound for the Queens stronghold. A neo-Nazi Anny, it was virtually taboo to city dwellers. The ride was a short one.

The small watcher waved a hand. The vehicle pulled away. He had pressed go.

I walked for a long hour. The rain had stopped. I saw buildings up ahead. A small cluster. I huddled to watch. *Observe before being observed.*

The earth was a soggy pulp. Rills of water sluiced against chipped pavement. Weeds, grasses grew shoulder high in the streets: a wasteland. The ruined buildings, lopsided and forlorn—victims, no doubt, of the *first* blight, after the Nazi-Soviet Victory Pact had splintered —seemed to stare back at me with sullen belligerence. I smelled wet grass, moist earth, rotting wood. A mosquito began to buzz— breakfast time in the insect world. I slapped at it. Something that looked like a cat had scurried across the street seconds before. There was no other movement.

I got up and began hiking again.

FLEISHER THREE

THE BUST-OUT

The trio jogged down the hallway like track stars whose heyday had been the Gay '90s. Slow but steady. It was a long, black, empty hallway. Their feet made sharp percussive sounds against the floor like beady-eyed toddlers working the hammer on mama's favorite table top. Echoes spun along the corridor, bounced off the walls. Earl was no great shakes at making time. It didn't seem to be his forte; he had heart, all right, but what he really needed was a pair of wheels. Still, Fleisher knew, this Earl wanted out as much as any of them—more, probably. He was giving it the old college try. That was cheering.

Earl Kneely puffed:

"It certainly is dandy seeing you boys. I hadn't counted on being sprung. 'No sir, old Earl,' I said to myself, 'your days are numbered. You've fallen on evil times. How far can the end be?' Yes sir, that's what I said to myself. The very words."

Lacy said:

"That's the crap, Earl. You shouldn't of worried. I wasn't gonna let you take no fall. What kinda pal you make me? Ain't we always been thick? Thick as thieves. Hee-hee."

Lacy was getting gay. The bust-out had gone to his noodle.

"All you hadda do," Lacy explained wisely, "was sit tight. Me and the sidekick here was bound to show."

"Well, that sure is mighty generous. I figured my goose was cooked. Those boys had me dead to rights, you know. Caught me with my pants down. In the act, so to speak. No sir, it don't pay to mess with that Kraft bunch. Those boys are bad eggs."

Lacy said:

"Just goes to show, don't it? Like I says to Eddy here soon's I get a line on what's happenin': 'Eddy,' I says, 'we gotta get Earl off the hook. He always shot square with me; he's a right guy; we gotta help him out.'"

"Well," Earl said, "I reckoned maybe in a pinch you might kind of look out for yourself."

"That's the bunk," Lacy said with great earnestness.

Eddy Fleisher said, "Have you no shame?"

"No," Lacy said.

Earl said, "That's certainly mighty generous."

They turned at the staircase, opened doors, started down steps.

Three men in hats and coats were coming up the steps. They didn't look like guards; they didn't look friendly either.

Both groups were waving dimmers, each spotlighting the other.

Darkness. Sudden and complete.

Lacy was first. Not wasting time, he dived back through the doorway. Fleisher felt him brush by.

Grabbing Earl by one thick arm, Eddy Fleisher heaved him up the four steps, pushed him into the hall.

Behind them bullets tore up the stairs.

"They're certainly not friendly," Earl wheezed.

"The bag!" Fleisher said to Lacy.

He said it more than once, all the while making tracks away from the doorway. The doorway was a menace. "The bag, you bastard," he hissed.

Lacy slowed down long enough to thrust the bag at him.

Earl, lost somewhere in the rear, sounded like a couple of elephants on the warpath.

Eddy Fleisher opened the bag, his legs still pumping.

Lacy complained from up ahead:

"You said no shootin'."

"I lied, you stinking crumb."

Fleisher's hand closed over a hard object. He called, "Earl."

"Righty-here." Fleisher had him fixed now. He pitched the block-buster past Kneely at the staircase door. It sailed off into the darkness like a model plane bearing a special surprise.

Eddy Fleisher suggested: "Run." He said it only once.

The patter of frenzied feet he immediately heard didn't belong to mice.

Fleisher didn't know if the door was open or closed; didn't know if the hall held people or not; his guess was not, but it was only a guess. He thought: How could they know we're all yellow-bellying it down the hall? If they used their heads, they'd be ducking now, afraid of bullets. He hoped they'd be using their heads; some people never do.

Behind them the hallway went blooey—rocked and splintered into small jagged pieces. They kept going.

"This sure won't put us in solid with Kraft," Kneely gasped.

Lacy concentrated on his leg-work; coat and all, he could tear up the turf when he had to; he was a real wing-ding.

Up ahead, a cross-corridor.

"Right," Eddy Fleisher called.

Right it was.

"Forget that," Fleisher said to Earl, who had moved up to within a foot of his elbow. "That angle's gone sour; you're dead and buried with Kraft anyway. Only that troupe didn't look like Kraft's stooges. Where were the uniforms?"

"Monkey business?" Kneely demanded.

"Why not? We probably did this joint a favor. An outside combo. Hell, they couldn't've been after us, could they?"

"Not too likely."

The trio ran on, turned a half-dozen corners. After a while, a door; a red light over it—the only light, it seemed, still in order. Underneath yellow letters spelled out:

EMERGENCY EXIT

Well, Fleisher thought, if this isn't an emergency, what is?

He called a halt.

Putting a shoulder to the metal made rusty hinges complain; the door groaned open like an old man prodded awake by a stick. Cold, damp air rushed in.

"Let's go," Fleisher said, shooing them through.

Metal steps climbed down the side of the building.

No moon, no company, nothing but the dark, dead night and the damp air. They went down.

Presently hard concrete was underfoot. The trio had stepped off the last rung: they had reached bottom. Some guys it takes a lifetime, but they'd done it quick.

"Where the shit are we?" Lacy asked.

"Still in one piece," Fleisher pointed out. "This is the far side of the plant. We go around."

Dark, bulky shapes of other plants hung to the northwest. United Tool covered a lot of ground, but it was padlocked for the night. All tumult and smoke a half-decade ago, the crash had put a real crimp in the company's style: it slept through most of the dark side now.

Following a concrete strip that circled the building, the trio swung around a corner. They had a surprise.

A squat, hatless man in a wide-belted raincoat, whose foot was planted on the Studebaker's right running board, jerked his head. Fleisher couldn't make out his face, but his voice, when he called, wouldn't have seemed pleasant even if it'd sounded like Kate Smith.

"Frank?" the voice said in a harsh whisper.

There was no Frank in this group.

Lacy shot him.

The man spun back into the night. All three dived for the car, tumbling into it helter-skelter. Fleisher hit the starter, the gun report still ringing in his ears.

Earl was saying, "Well, well, well." His tone summed up the situation, but the words were still a bit optimistic. None of this had been on Fleisher's program; it was an added feature—a short one, he hoped. The car lurched ahead, headlights probing.

The plant's side door popped open; a tall, lanky don pranced out, a tommy gun bobbing in his gloved hands. Hot metal poured from its snout.

By that time the car was well on its way. Fleisher was sweating.

"The racket's turned wicked, all right," Earl said with a sigh; he'd ducked to the floor.

"It's sure no pip," Lacy agreed, also from the floor.

Fleisher aimed the car toward the gates, opened her up. They sped through the night, wheels roaring in turn over concrete, tar, and gravel.

Lights shimmered ahead through the swirling fog:

The gates.

The figure dancing before them, in cap and uniform, was waving his arms frantically.

"Wants us to stop," Earl pointed out.

"Sure looks that way," Fleisher conceded.

Putting his foot on the gas pedal, Eddy Fleisher pressed down hard. The Studebaker almost grew wings. The engine screamed like a patient under the knife with no anesthetic. Wind pummeled doors and windows. The leather seat rose and sank under them, making the trio rattle around like dice on a gaming table. The edge was theirs; they'd put a half-nelson on the night and had it reeling.

Eddy Fleisher heard himself laugh.

His hand swept down on the horn, held it there. He wanted the gateman to get the idea. He got it. His frenzied leap took him out of harm's way, away from plummeting hood and into dark foliage bordering the road. The gate itself, nothing more than fancy slats of wood, folded against headlights like papier-mâché, was left scattered in large and small chunks across the roadway.

Rolling fields sprawled to right and left. Brooklyn was as empty here as a hobo's lunch-box. Widely-spaced lamp posts made soft yellow circles in the night. Telegraph wires angled off into the distance.

Fleisher drove away from there.

Soon small two- and three-story houses began springing up, multiplied, started to fill whole blocks: the residential section. Cutting corners, Fleisher doubled back, criss-crossed the side streets.

He turned to Earl, offered a grin and congratulations. "Where to?" he asked.

Earl was busy mopping his face with a large red and polka-dot hanky. There was a lot to mop. "I certainly do appreciate this," he said, and kept repeating it with a number of variations until he was sure the point had been made.

Trolley tracks rumbled under wheels; frame cottages began to be replaced by larger structures: office buildings and lofts. Downtown Brooklyn lay dead ahead.

Earl said hopefully, "You can just drop me off anywhere around here, boys; I'll be running along home. No sense putting you to more trouble, is there?" Good manners mitigated against this proposal. Eddy Fleisher said as much.

"No, eh?" Kneely said.

"No," Fleisher said.

Lacy agreed.

Earl Kneely sighed. "Well, I really won't forget all the help you boys've been to me. No, sir."

Eddy Fleisher assured him he wouldn't.

"Well, that is wonderful," Earl said.

"The swag," Fleisher said.

Earl, rubbing his chubby hands together, tried to look puzzled. "What about it? The deal's still on. Of course it is. Sure." He seemed eager to let them know this.

"You bet the deal's still on," Lacy said.

"Only more so," Fleisher added.

Earl tried a chuckle. "A bonus, huh? Well, I can't say you boys don't have it coming."

"Uh-uh," Eddy Fleisher said.

"Uh-uh?" Earl said. He put feeling into it.

"Nope," Fleisher said. "It's a three-way split now."

"Three-way," Earl repeated.

"Uh-huh," Fleisher said. "Three-way."

"Yes," Earl said. "Of course, if that's what you boys think best."

"That's it, all right," Lacy said.

Earl sighed. "Three ways."

"Tonight," Lacy said.

"Tonight, boys?"

"Now," Fleisher said.

"Well," Earl said, "I'll level with you fellas. It would be kind of hard to get the stuff right this instant—if you know what I mean?"

"No," Fleisher said, "I don't. Maybe you ought to tell us."

"Yeah," Lacy said. "Tell us."

Earl cleared his throat. "Well, it's like this, boys. The stuff, you know, it's sort of in safe-keeping."

"I'm glad to hear that," Fleisher said. "I wouldn't want any of it getting lost."

"Oh no," Earl said. "That wouldn't happen. No sir. Boys—I'll tell you what. We split in the morning. Three ways, just like you say. Three ways. A deal?" making it sound as if he was offering them the Hope diamond at a discount.

Eddy Fleisher laughed at him.

Tom Lacy, taking a large, ugly pistol out of a coat pocket, cradled it on his lap.

Fleisher said, "Earl buddy, you've been trimming them blind; you've beat them out of so much at the Tool Works that they finally wised up to you. Greed, Earl, is a mean trait in a man. But you can shake it, pal; we're with you, we'll help you."

"Well," Earl said, "that is mighty white of you." He didn't sound terribly cheerful, but then he'd had a rough night.

"We divvy now," Fleisher explained.

Earl sighed. "Now."

"That's the tune I was waiting for," Fleisher said happily. "I know the words to that one."

"Hell," Lacy said, "we swung the job, Earl; we saved your ass. You ain't gonna hold out on us now, are you?"

"Not me, boys."

"Tom's right," Fleisher said. "There's no sense in hogging the roll. There'd be no future in it."

Earl sighed again:

"Yes, sir," he said, "I think you boys've convinced me."

"I figured we might," said Fleisher.

"Yes," Kneely said, "your argument is certainly persuasive."

"That's swell," Eddy Fleisher said earnestly. "I wouldn't have wanted all this effort to go to waste."

NORTON FOUR

THE CITY

Staring into the darkness of the tunnel, I tried to remember:

The Cope-Con. My escape and dash through the countryside. The ride I'd hitched with the trucker.

I seemed to recall all of it, and yet I couldn't get over the feeling that there were still holes, that my mind was somehow incomplete.

The outposters. No help there and I'd gone on . . .

The sloots! Which somehow I'd bested, eluded. *How?*

I'd forgotten most of the raid, even escaping with Dr. Knox, until the voice had jogged my memory. *What was it?*

I wondered: Other-Worlders? Could this voice be one of their products? The OWs were a small mystical sect specializing in illusions of the mind, a temporary escape from the pressures of the work-oriented Annys. Well endowed, but not all that widespread. A sanctioned heresy cutting across three Annys.

The tech-ers, who had set up the OW temple, were Copes. So I knew that all the OW mind devices built into the temple had a mechanical basis: before the wonders took place, a switch had to be flicked.

But what would they be doing here?

So perhaps this was something else . . . Either way, I was back full circle. Alone with a voice.

The voice said, "Well, why *are* you standing there? Walk on . . . it's *perfectly* safe."

Placing one foot carefully in front of the other, I began moving ahead. I'd gotten no more than two yards when the voice said, "Over here."

It seemed to come from the ground.

I bent down. Loose earth covered the floor; my fingers began sifting through it, closed over a small, round object, cold to the touch.

The voice said, "Ah!"

My hand froze, as if some enchantment had turned it to marble.

"Well?" the voice said impatiently.

"What do I do now?"

"Lift me."

I did.

Light flared. Bright, blinding light.

"Contact flare," the bubble explained. "It's nothing." Instantly the light began to dim; the voice sighed, "It won't last very long, I'm afraid."

I peered at the thing. A perfect sphere, larger than a marble but not by much. Almost no weight. The voice seemed to come from somewhere in its center. But there was nothing to see.

Perfectly transparent. Some kind of crystal . . . perhaps.

I pulled my eyes away, to look around in the fading light.

I was in a tunnel. The walls, cracked; the ceiling—high above—in pieces. The mound of earth through which I'd entered was visible, a neat pile, at one end. The light began to sputter. I saw I was on a platform, corroded metal rails below me. Faint lettering decorated the right wall; it read: 86th St.

The voice spoke. "We are in the old Lexington Avenue IRT station. Once trains ran here, although you will no doubt find that difficult to believe. We are on the uppermost of two levels. This one is blocked by a landslide further along. We must go below. It should take us clear to your city—if that, my dear fellow, is still your objective . . ."

I said it was.

"I was afraid it might be. We had best hurry. The light is almost exhausted. The stairs are behind you."

"This will take some getting used to," I said.

"Bubbles make fine company," the bubble said. "You'll see."

Mid-morning.

I emerged from the tunnel blinking in the bright sunlight. I moved out cautiously, trying to take in all directions. It looked all right—at least, no hostile movement; even the city sounds didn't carry this far. I saw rubble, the remains of tall buildings, now crushed, battered, some virtually pulverized. The city itself was still some half-mile distant. Here the ground was raw and pitted. Skeletal structures that had once been buildings leaned precariously at impossible angles. Fifty-foot piles of loose stone, brick, concrete rose skyward. Wind scattered particles in the air. Bushes and even trees sprouted from the earth that yearly made greater inroads on the shattered pavement.

The street sign, as if in mockery, still stood stiffly at attention. It read:

TIMES SQUARE

By carefully climbing one of the rubble piles I could gaze over the wasted area. It seemed peaceful enough.

Diagonally across from me was the giant statue—once ten stories tall, the symbol of its age, now resting on its side amid the junk and litter. Green mold disfigured its surface; rust peeked out from under the mold. Here lay the founding fathers, now expurgated from most —but not all—Anny texts. Side by side they rested, their metal arms twined around each other's shoulders as if pledging their eternal comradeship.

Hitler and Stalin.

I looked away. The city sparkled dead ahead.

The bubble said, "I scan no one—we are in luck."

Luck? It was something I could hardly imagine. My clothes hung in tatters. Dirt, grime, earth covered me. Rills of sweat ran down my body, made long, crooked lines over my darkened skin. My mouth felt powdery. A hammer seemed to beat inside my head. Hands and feet shook with palsied exhaustion. A mild breeze might send me spinning, toppling.

"A clear field," the bubble said enthusiastically from inside my shirt pocket. "Certainly no sloots in evidence."

"They don't usually come this far," I managed to whisper. "The wardens use them for target practice."

"Eh?"

"You'll see. As soon as we get closer."

"You mean . . . my dear fellow . . . that they will shoot at us?"

"No," I said wearily, "they'll shoot at *me*."

"Oh dear . . ."

"If," I said, "they spot me."

"There is no one here," the bubble assured me. "It's perfectly safe. I'll scan, you know."

"I know."

At first my mind kept reverting to the bubble's riddle. Exasperatingly, it had taxed my powers of concentration. The basic possibilities were circumscribed: Anny, Heresy—one or the other. But within these categories the possibilities multipled staggeringly: no end to either. A clue? None. Given sufficient transmission power, the broadcast—for what else could it be?—might come from almost any zoning on the eastern seaboard. A new science, perhaps. But Anny sovereignty had crippled communication: there was no way of knowing what the various Tech-ers were up to. And for each spy network, an elaborate counter-system existed. The Copes, who recruited their members across the board, from all Annys, might be expected to know. Apparently they didn't. If there'd been any talk, it had eluded me. New York-New Jersey zonings were Copes hunting grounds. Copes didn't figure much beyond that. Who could tell? Somewhere, somehow, bubbles of this type might even be a commonplace. That was understandable. What wasn't, what made no sense at all, was *my* involvement . . .

After a while I gave it up.

Putting one foot before the next began to absorb all of my attention. I could worry about bubbles later—if there was a later. My troubles began to seem so perverse, so overwhelming, my ruin so complete, that the bubble became a secondary concern. It couldn't make matters much worse, could it? And they weren't going to get any better. I'd made too many blunders for that. This time around, I wasn't going to come out ahead. The bubble itself didn't seem too stable either, appeared rattle-brained, somewhat erratic. How could I rely on it? How could I rely on *anything*? My error had been in taking on too much, in overextending myself. And before that, the Cope-Con itself: I'd turned a deaf ear to the warnings. And why had I listened to Knox of all people? There would have been more safety in numbers . . .

I stumbled.

The terrain seemed to quake under me, to jiggle and shimmy. Like a roll of jelly. *Nerves.* Part of me still remained watchful, alert: signs of life were inimical here. Another part no longer cared.

The bubble said, "We are about to encounter a brown-clad warden."

"Coalition." I said it automatically. And thought wildly: *The bubble's an outzoner!*

Everyone within miles knew that Brown was Coalition.

But what interest could an outzoner possibly have in the city? *Or me?*

"Look," I complained. "I'm in no shape to outrun a warden."

"Tell me about the brown ones."

"Tell you what?"

"Anything you want. What is their . . . er . . . slant?"

I sighed. "Well, the Coalition believes in the dignity of human labor. Except that all Annys, I suppose, believe in something like that. The Brownies have a triumvirate at the top. So Alldeck—that's their think-text—must have been for that. He's against retirement. He feels women ought to work as hard as men. He likes to see kids working, too. Coalition brown means a rotten life. Worse than some other Annys perhaps. But a life at least."

"Their Anny is inferior to *your* Anny?" the bubble wanted to know.

"Well, the League's got the Incest Cult; I'd say that's something in its favor, wouldn't you? Actually, the League's a holiday by comparison. But that's not saying much. Look, perhaps you'd better tell me your plan."

Abruptly, we had reached the brink of the city. No transition, no sculptured lawns. Waste and ruin. Then the climbing walls of the great manors. Here the structures were brown, but gold was visible westward, and green to the east.

"There is only a solitary warden here," the bubble said. "I scan many out on the walks, but beyond this building . . . at this cross-section, there is only one."

"You've spotted a traffic warden. So what?"

"Where he is, there are too many pedestrians . . . it would be unwise to take action against him there . . . we must summon him *here*."

I coughed up a desperate laugh. "Look," I said. "It's all I can do to stand up. You expect me to tackle a real live warden?"

"My dear Norton," the bubble explained, "I shall arrange it."

"You do other things besides talk?"

"Talk will be enough. You must leave certain matters to me."

"Why should I? What have you done except talk? Who are you? I don't even know *that*. Look, don't expect miracles. I'm stuck or I wouldn't have gone this far with you. I'm not out to get myself killed. It's nothing to you—you're just a voice. But I'm the glink who gets it in the neck if there's trouble. All these tricks with wardens are fine—only I'm not the man for them. Look at my hands . . . look at them. They won't keep still for a second. I can't control my own hands anymore; how am I going to beat up a warden? You think anyone can just walk up to those glinks and knock them over? What's wrong with you?"

The bubble said, "There is nothing wrong with *me*, my dear fellow. We'll use subterfuge. There is a piece of pipe some forty yards to your left. It is partially buried, by the boulder . . . you see? Pick it up. You'll be glad."

"I'll be dead," I said, but I stumbled away to pick it up.

"There is an alley that opens onto the walk," the bubble continued. "We shall make use of it. Momentarily, it is deserted. You will hide in a doorway. I will project my voice and summon the warden."

I said, "He won't come."

"He'll come," the bubble assured me. "I will speak to him as a father to a son, and while we are deep in conversation, you, my dear fellow, will step out and hit him over the head."

"Just like that?"

"Precisely."

"He'll kill me."

"You'll hit him *hard*."

I said, "Think of something else."

"See here, Norton . . . you can't go running through the streets looking like that. You require decent apparel."

"Why pick on a warden? I'd rather hit an ordinary anny; it's less trouble. Wardens carry weapons, they hit back."

"We need a warden."

"Maybe you do."

"*I* don't need anything," the bubble said testily.

The alleyway was no more than a narrow pavement between two manors. Crouched in a doorway, I sweated in plain misery, feeling as capable and fearless as a one-armed panhandler up against the court gladiator. In my unsteady hands I gripped the pipe as though it were a lifeline to some better, more hopeful place.

"Put me down now," the bubble urged, "toward the street entrance. About twenty feet should do."

"I'd better say good-by," I said.

"Why, my dear fellow?"

"If this doesn't work, I won't get a chance."

Rolling the bubble toward the mouth of the alley, I sank back in my hiding place. The cry "Alldeck excretes!" seemed to fill the passage. I thought: Some lungs, then realized the ineptness of the phrase. One bellow was enough. The warden came racing in, deserting his traffic post. The bubble had been right; the warden was alone. The passing annys had not paid the slightest attention to the deadly insult. But the warden had. It was his job.

He lunged blindly past the bubble, only to hear it scream:

"Work is excrement!"

I was shaking in my doorway. Outright heresy does that to me sometimes. That and total physical funk.

The warden, a brown-clad, heavy-set glink, pivoted a gun in his large hand. His eyes raked the alleyway.

"Down here," the bubble called, "the bright shiny object."

The warden glanced down at his feet.

"That's right," the bubble said.

The warden stared, open-mouthed.

I crept out of my doorway.

"Life was meant for play," the bubble was saying earnestly. "Only a dimwit like Alldeck would fail to appreciate that." Rage flushed the warden's face. He aimed his gun.

I brought the pipe down on his head. The warden fell down.

"See?" the bubble said. "He was sincerely interested in hearing my opinions . . . Don't forget me," it called as I dragged the Brownie into the doorway. I retrieved my marble and began stripping the warden.

The bubble said, "The weapon will be useful. The uniform will go unchallenged. I was quite correct in my prognosis. There's a public washroom down the block. Use it."

Along the walks was no place to procrastinate. I didn't. A glink in warden's costume might expect hardship at any and all turns. Disorder could settle like a plague, would be sure to involve him, entangle him in duties that might last for hours.

The bubble said, "Go!" I went.

I beat a very hasty retreat through the brown-hued streets, marked by the haste and anxiety that characterized Brownies. No one gave me a second glance. Why should they? Soon the brown towers were thankfully behind me. I headed southeast now toward the gold sector—the League—speeding down the free-walk.

The sign said:

FATHER PEN HEARTILY RECOMMENDS THE INCEST CULT

Father Pen's broad face, enlarged a hundredfold, wagged at the streaming crowd below; in his extended hand bobbed a pair of nude lovers. The voice-over said, "The League's right, by god!" repeating the slogan over and over. The Pen-aids were strategically spaced every few blocks. Pen meant index.

"Green! Green! Green!" the Alliance poster shrilled. "Green for index, green for sheen! Live Alliance! Be bald!" The poster flexed a huge 3-D biceps. A giant finger beckoned.

"Fed blue is good for you," the spinning globe prattled. "More annys have switched to blue than any other Anny. Why not you? Proven quality; quality counts."

The dancing girls chorused, "Silver! Silver! Silver! Corporation means silver," raising a plastic leg in unison. "A silver life!"

The writhing statue on the cross intoned, "Willgear saves you. Willgear brings comfort. Willgear heals."

Only you couldn't switch, I knew, because it would be a terrible black mark against you, because it could take months to process your case, while your rejected Anny sought revenge, erased you from its rolls, hung you in limbo, or simply made you vanish, an un-anny, a blank on each and every Anny roll.

It was all puffery.

"Poetry, a sanctioned heresy," the lips smiled. They were nine feet across, projected from a high, pointed tower. Stripes of yellow and black spiraled the tower's length. A flower repeatedly blossomed through the open lips. Its petals waved. The flower explained, "Meet like spirits." The voice-over sang: "Sanctioned, sanctioned, sanctioned."

"Forget with Nod," the male image said earnestly. "Be a hooker in your off-time. Forget time. Hookers are sanctioned."

"Sanctioned. Sanctioned. Sanctioned," screamed the game-parlor-aids; "Sanctioned," screamed the inter-Anny eat-stands; "Sanctioned," screamed the fun-rooms, the play dens . . .

The free-walk buzzed with activity. Uniforms abounded, pedestrians from all Annys streamed along.

The sound rose from the blue sector. Like a roaring wave, breaking over the free-walk. Activity—for an instant—seemed to petrify, to freeze in mid-stride.

"Trouble up ahead," the bubble warned in half-whisper, its voice projecting from my buttoned breast pouch.

Elbowing my way along, I stepped into a drug mart. There was no time for principle.

"Two grams of lift-o," I said.

The clerk shook white pills from a slender orange container as I paid out the index, took and swallowed the tablets. Turning, I went back onto the free-walk. Two miles to League manor. The blue sector lay between.

The crowd was moving again—uneasily. An awkward restlessness seemed to have seized it. Trouble in the blue sector. Trouble. Trouble. Trouble.

"Move quickly," the bubble urged, "we can still get by. But hurry."

Lift-o surged through body, arms and legs, accelerated my pulse; muscles tightened, a spring came to my step. Lift-o would carry me, lift-o would give me strength. Later I would pay, but now I was held aloft in a state of perpetual—death-defying—lift.

I used my shoulder to make room, wedged my way onto the free-walk center. Away from the stands and attractions there was less congestion. I quickened my pace. The cries from the blue sector were clearer now, more distinct—trouble, trouble, trouble. They swelled into a wild roar, a roar that shook the free-walk. Fear pinched the crowd face, anxiety ravaged it. In an instant there woud be panic—there *was* panic.

"The mall," the bubble cried.

Lift-o urged me on; forearms and shoulder scattered the crowd before me. I began to run.

Other wardens those in gold, silver, green, blue, brown uniforms —ran for their posts, made a bee-line for their sector, some already unbuckling their weapons, drawing their lasers, stunners, projectiles.

The siren began to wail.

The free-walk broke into small, galloping clusters; the crowd splintered in milling confusion, alarm. A contingent of flush-faced, laughing, eager blood-watchers cut for the blue sector, intent on seeing what kill there was. Others sought cover. The eat-stands were closing up. The fun rooms and game parlors rolled down their protective awnings. Steel panels slid smoothly over display windows, store fronts, snapping shut. The sirens, now ringing the free-walk, throbbed and moaned over the heads of the scattering crowds. "Shelter, shelter, shelter," mechanical voices trilled. Red, white, blue safety-tunnel-aids winked and flashed a thousand flaring light bulbs; metal fingers grasped the offered index, rolling-walks—helter-skelter —propelled the safety-seekers underground, out of harm's way. The foam-rooms waited, sealed against chaos from without.

I took the gold mall.

The elevated sliding malls—all sectors—branched out like tentacles over the free-walk, slanted off toward their respective Annys.

Below me the blue sector bustled.

A full-scale riot was in progress; it boiled and bubbled among the blue buildings, driving the wardens back. From my vantage point, the mob resembled nothing so much as toy figures, their springs busted, out of control. But riding the mall exposed me to laser and projectile blast; I shrank back, squinting ahead toward the sparkling gold towers in the distance.

A fat party huddling next to me mopped his brow with a yellow and black tissue: poetry heresy. Turning worried eyes toward me, he spoke, and not in rhyme either. "Third one in two days, neighbor. Bread riot. It's a bad one, all right, worst I've seen. What's the world coming to, neighbor?"

Wardens were scurrying through the League sector, ringing the League palace and manor gateways, posting themselves around zone entrance and exit points, blocking off the free-walk promenade. Their gold uniforms electro-creased, sharp, immaculate. Their weapons—here in League center—still holstered. There was relative calm.

Faces—chattering, straining—jammed manor windows; balconies creaked under massed onlookers, all magnifiers focused on the blue zone.

"League annys," a voice crooned, "remain in your quarters; do not venture out onto the walks unless it is absolutely necessary. Remain calm. League wardens are at the ready; League wardens protect you." The voice—mellow, soothing—drifted through the League sector, amplified by a hundred speakers. The streets were emptying.

Striding through the 12th manor-gateway, I found myself in the familiar arched, golden lobby. Annys went about their business here unhurriedly, their steps clicking and echoing on the gold marbled flooring.

Banners of Lancaster, Brandon, Father Pen, Joe Dermus, fluttered from ceiling and walls. *Lacers* all.

Shops lined ground-level, layouts shimmering behind show windows: food and clothing marts, registered microfilmed and audioed Learneries, utility and pleasure dens. Here uniforms swarmed. Wardens from all the Annys, their duties extending beyond policing, mingled and met. Unnoticed in the crowd, I went my solitary way.

A speed-rise at the northwest lobby rode me up to the 106th level.

Stepping out into an empty corridor, I thought, *Of course:* bread riots pulled the customers, had an irresistible appeal. They'd be at windows and balconies.

An advantage.

For they knew me here—by name, by sight. They'd know at once that I had no right to the brown uniform. And they'd give me away without a second's thought or regret.

Behind me the wall-sign glimmered:

LEAGUE

SUB-GROUP

INCEST CULT

No sealed stamp on Nina's and my rooming. I held the medallion cross-lock—tensing for the alarm that might, that *should* come, but didn't—and watched the door slide open.

The wide bed was draped in fresh linen. Open green curtains across wall windows exposed sunlight and gold towers. The tell-viewer was dark. In the adjoining chamber desks, chairs, and table were in order. The freeze-box in the food den was still stocked, the minute-cook spotless, the rinse self-polishing. The wardrobe hooks still held our clothing.

There was no sign of Nina.

Neither voc-message nor note. The rooming seemed unlived-in.

Examining the premises minutely, I could find no tell-tale spy probe, no indication that the dwelling had in any way been tampered with.

The bubble said, "Well?" I'd almost forgotten about the bubble.

"I don't know."

"Believe me," the bubble said, "we have no time. She's obviously gone. This is a place of disorder . . . perhaps she has sought shelter elsewhere. In any case, you cannot remain here."

"You're right about that," I agreed.

"As I've indicated, the lab—"

"I'll find her first."

"My dear Norton, why do you persist in this suicide wish?"

"You're wasting your breath."

"Bubbles have no breath," the bubble said.

Over the call-box a woman at Nina's office told me that Nina had failed to report for work during the last three days. The bureau had no idea where the girl was. I tried Brent with similar results: no answer at his rooming and listed AWOL at the League Archives for the third day in a row.

After I showered, grabbed a quick bite, changed into civvies, and popped a lift-o into my mouth, I proceeded to interview the tenants of the adjoining roomings. They could tell me nothing. Nina's comings and goings, if any, had gone unobserved. I learned one thing: my neighbors were still unaware of my posting. All this mayhem had bought me time.

I stuck a laser into a pocket, decided against contacting any of the Cope underground through the call-box apparatus—that would be begging for the lock-up—and took the speed-descend down to the lobby. Altogether I had spent less than an hour in the dwelling. I didn't think I'd ever see it again. I wasn't sorry.

An ordinary enough structure. An out-manor Alliance dwelling. Old, neglected. Green towers rose some blocks away, but here was the shabby domain of Alliance ne'er-do-wells, the hangers-on. Not many persons were about.

I began to cross the street, then thought better of it. I stepped back into the alley. No need to take chances; I had the bubble. "Safe across there?" I asked.

There was a profound silence.

I repeated my question. Nothing.

Removing the thing from my pocket pouch, I glared at it. "Say something!" I said.

A voice from behind me laughed.

Whirling, I saw a scraggly derelict seated on the asphalt, grinning rakishly at me. "Coochy-coo," he said. "Playing with marbles, sonny?"

I left the alleyway in disgust, crossed the street and entered the three-story ramshackle dwelling.

An old crone on the first floor responded to my knock.

"Ain't here," she said. "Oliver moved out last week." Oliver was my Cope contact. "You better go," the old woman warned. I took her advice.

Back on the street, I made tracks for the blue zone. There were back alleys and narrow passageways that might offer protection. I used them. Nina, Brent and I had a second, more secluded rooming in the tenement section of the Blueies. Only index could buy privacy here. It would be the place to go if trouble materialized. No call-box connected this dwelling with the outside world; I'd have to put in a personal appearance. Too bad about the riot; it would complicate things. But by this time I was used to complications.

Trotting through the almost-empty streets, I could hear the sounds of violence growing louder, more distinct. I felt rotten. Lift-o letdown? I had used lift-o before, but never with such disastrous results. There was nothing to do but go on.

Again and again I found myself anxiously addressing the bubble. Stony silence was my reward. There could be no doubt of it now: the bubble had deserted me. How was it possible? I felt betrayed. Cast out. *Alone.*

And the nightmare was beginning again.

The narrow, twisted streets and dilapidated buildings seemed to call to me, seemed to jeer and threaten, their words a jumble but their meaning unmistakable.

And the echo of their screams rang in my ears.

I stood frozen, paralyzed by indecision, Nina's image springing up before me. I longed to turn from the blue sector, to scramble back the way I'd come and leave the city. An almost irresistible desire. I ignored it.

I moved on again.

Mere movement, somehow, made me feel better.

The first body I came to was that of a young girl, the dead eyes rolled up in their white sockets as if in derision at what had been done to her. The broken mouth seemed to grin up at me, a mute testimony to the uselessness of all endeavors. She still wore the silver armband designating Corporation.

The discoveries of the second, third, and fourth bodies followed in quick succession.

Rounding a corner, I saw a couple dozen annys coming out of a side street. More followed them, too many to count. A lone figure raced before them: a blue-clad warden.

Not this way, I almost shouted.

I made for a doorway. Bless those doorways!

They cut down the warden almost at my feet. The crowd came.

I stepped out and became part of it. A foot kicked the dead Blueie. Lips grinned. Voices laughed. I saw red, green, yellow, and silver armbands. Women were among this crowd. Someone pointed back up the block. The mob spilled over in that direction. I went with it.

They were headed the right way at least. Five more blocks would see me almost to the brownstone building. My destination.

The thin, wiry woman next to me swore. "Scum," she spat, her eyes bulging, "that's all they are, those wardens—scum!"

Two blocks north and a voice crackled over the mob's head:

"Drop your arms."

A loudspeaker blared:

"Remain perfectly still. Do not move. This is riot control speaking. Repeat—"

The mob moved, came alive, bursting like a grenade in all directions.

A squad of wardens faced us up ahead on the walk; to our rear a second squad appeared.

The air, suddenly, was thick with smoke, gun shots, laser beams. The thin woman at my side gurgled and fell down bleeding. Crouching, I used my laser to open a storefront window—a cleaning parlor. Glass shattered and fell away. I stepped over the sill. Behind me, activity rose to fever pitch, wounded and dying screamed and raved. I moved fast now, leaping over a counter, brushing aside a yellow curtain. I was in a back room. Clothing racks. Hands and shoulders sent them spilling. The door leading to the alley was locked. My laser cut the lock like a razor through soft cheese.

Outside, propellers whirled. Riot copters. I raced away. Going over a wooden fence, I found myself in a courtyard; cobblestones led to a high gate. I went over it. A hissing sound behind me. Gas. It quilted walks and houses, settled over the crowd I had left seconds before.

I let myself in through a side door and followed a set of back stairs to the first floor. The three-chamber rooming I entered, off a side corridor, was immaculate. And empty. I examined the freezer. Half bare. During the last week it had been fully stocked.

I went down to the ground floor. Max Gordon was in the kitchen, seated on a stool, watching his wife Rea working over the minute-cook. Gordon, a large beefy man close to sixty, wore a white T-shirt and dark flared slacks; a walrus mustache curved over his upper lip. He rose to shake hands. The woman at the stove, short, narrow-faced, with black hair tied back in a bow, bobbed her head twice in greeting. Gordon nodded me to a chair, lit a cigar and said, "Your woman was here."

"His sister," Rea said primly.

"Never could get used to that," the round-faced Gordon admitted. "Mighty pretty little woman though."

"Isn't natural," Rea said.

"Each Anny got its way," Gordon said.

"When was she here?" I asked.

"You remember?" Gordon said to his wife.

She turned her gray eyes away from the stove. "All of three days ago."

"Brent?" I asked.

"Not him," the woman said, going back to her work.

"You worried about him and the sister, huh? Figure they went the slam?" Gordon grinned good-naturedly.

"I'm worried," I said, "but not about that."

"The Annys," Gordon said thoughtfully. "I guess they're a big let-down."

"Rot," Rea said. "They're rot."

Gordon sighed, "They don't provide a good life no more."

"They never did," his wife said.

"We're all worried," Gordon said.

"Worried sick," the woman said. "It's a crying shame."

"They can't keep the peace even," Gordon said. "That most of all. All these years we've been wide on the think; should've shucked the line long ago."

"Look," I said. "Did she say where she was going?"

"Your sister? I guess she did. You remember, Ma?"

The woman said three words, "The Pen estate."

"That's right," Gordon said. "That's it. She was going to see Father Pen. Or something like that. Isn't that right, Ma?"

"Right as rain. That's what she said anyhow."

"She didn't say why," I asked, "did she?"

"Not a word. She only stayed a short while."

"Maybe fifteen minutes," Rea said.

"What is it, son?" Gordon asked. "You lose her? Figure she jumped the clutch?"

"I don't know," I said.

"His own sister," Rea said.

"Trouble," Gordon said. "There's trouble everywhere."

Trouble found me less than a block from the brownstone.

First noise, then the noisemakers. By that time, I was under an archway. Wardens were coming—about ten of them and at their heels a mob. It was becoming a familiar sight. Incredible, but the revolt had gone much further than anyone could reasonably have expected. The food shortage had done it, had lit the spark, had brought the annys together as nothing else could. It was still fantastic.

Bending double, I made myself small. There was nothing in presenting a large target to these people. I preferred that they shoot each other rather than me. Soon they might go away.

More wardens came trotting out of a crosswalk; these seemed far better armed than their fleeing colleagues. At least three squads. Dismayed, I realized that a pitched battle was about to take place.

I squirmed around for the first time to see where I was. Sheets of metal covered windows and doorways; no cracks or gaps. The neighborhood had prepared for the worst.

The worst came:

Bullets and lasers competed for attention. Laser beams hissed and sizzled into the crowd. Bullets bit, tore and chewed into pavement, doorways, bodies, and vehicles.

Two new squads of wardens had long automatic weapons. They used them. The block was semi-residential; clusters of three- and four-story brownstones were punctuated by three seven-story blue manors; a half-dozen storefronts, closed and shuttered, faced the street.

More wardens sprang up at both ends of the block. Three or four hundred rampaging annys filled the pavements.

Down walk a window edged open. Metal gleamed through the opening: a laser. Its beam caught a blue-clad warden from behind. More windows came open now; doorways began to fill with crouching figures.

The local annys, I saw, were taking a hand in the fracas.

The wardens had seen it too, were starting slowly to back off.

A man planted on a brownstone rooftop used a machine-gun. A chimney gave him cover as he let loose at the wardens below.

Panic began to break warden ranks. One frantically tried to run a broken field down-walk toward safety. He fell.

A familiar figure. I saw Gordon. He'd chosen a rooftop, but prudently, one adjoining his own brownstone. Down on his belly, he had a shotgun in his hands. A wild grin was spread across his face. It vanished under cover.

Someone tossed a grenade. Part of a brownstone went up in the air like shredded paper.

I crawled out into the street; reinforcements were bound to arrive sooner or later. It all depended on what the rest of the city was up to; if the contagion had spread to the other quarters, help might never arrive for the wardens here. But there was no certainty to my guesses. Gas copters might materialize at any instant. Wisdom lay in retreat. I crept under a vehicle, looked down the block. Feet. Hundreds of feet. Stomping, shifting, anxious feet. The view left something to be desired. Edging forward, I saw that the feet were attached to legs, the legs to torsos.

Smoke came—rolling waves of it; lasers cut white startling lines through it. Men writhed and fell in the smoke—screaming, wild-eyed, incoherent.

I began crawling back to my archway. This was no place for an innocent bystander.

As I waited, huddled, laser in hand, sounds began to alter in pitch and character, to assume dimensions of a bedlam rather than a war. Noises of combat diminished. Only the cries of the wounded were left.

After a while I went back onto the walk.

Storefronts, buildings, and general scenery were a riddled and charred mess—a cross between a vandal's daydream and a general's delight. The results were far less satisfactory for the participants. Most were just so much chopped meat now. Others dragged themselves around on broken, lacerated bodies. Puddled blood was in plentiful supply.

The attack from the houses—the neighborhood residents joining the rebels—had momentarily confused the wardens, had driven them off. But they'd be back; I was sure of that. And this time they'd come in proper numbers.

What would they do?

Mop up the remnants still loitering on the walks? No doubt. Would they also raze the brownstones, declare war on their own annys?

Whatever they did, things would never quite be the same again. Even if they put the pieces together, this time it would spell out something else, something unimaginable, perhaps unthinkable.

My hand slipped to my pocket. Another lift-o? You could flap off with lift-o, shake up your mind like a scrambled egg. It would be one too many. Better do without. I wondered if I ought to check on Gordon, see if he and Rea were all right.

There was no time.

If I meant to save myself, to find Nina, I'd have to get out now while I still had the chance.

I began to run. Again.

INTERMISSION

The man in the shadows still fidgeted on his three-legged stool in the corner.

The red neon light had winked out by this time; the cars and trolleys had fled the darkened avenues and byways, which were now the province of solitary night. Only the lone foghorn still crooned over the waterfront, and an occasional el rumbled along as if in this way asserting its claim over the empty streets.

"I don't get it, Eddy," he said.

The man with the gun said, "What's that? What don't you get?"

"How'd you turn up in this?"

"That's what you want?"

"I wouldn't mind."

"Okay," Eddy Fleisher said. "I'll tell you where it began."

FLEISHER FOUR

THE PRIVATE EYE

Fingers drummed on the window pane.

Eddy Fleisher, in the other room, saw that it was 9:15. He had spent the day here in his Madison Avenue digs, his sometimes home whenever he hit the big town. A five-room spread in a four-story townhouse. He put down the Evening Sun. Beatrice Lillie worked the gags on WJZ; he turned her off, padded into the bedroom, and slid open the window. A fire escape ran down to the courtyard below.

"You've got some queer habits," Fleisher said when Felix Berger crawled through the window.

"You ought to see me when I'm lushed up," Berger said with equanimity.

He followed Fleisher into the next room, took off his hat, coat and scarf, flinging them onto the couch. Berger sank into an easy chair, adjusting the sharp creases of his trousers.

Berger was a redhead, about thirty-five, slim and of medium height. He lit a thin, baby-sized cigar after Fleisher poured out the hootch, and arranged himself in the armchair. His eyes lazily took in the surroundings.

He said, "You're looking flush, Eddy." And grinned.

"Well, I can't complain."

"Yeah. Still with Kraft?"

"Sure. Whaddja think?"

"Enjoying it?"

He shrugged. "It's all right."

"It's a living, huh?"

"It's a living."

"Yeah," Felix Berger said. "You hit this burg much, Eddy?"

"Every now and then."

"Do a lot of travelin', do you?"

"Come on, Felix, let's cut the crap. You know I do. What's on your mind?"

"I just mean would they know you around town?"

"Know me? Yeah, I guess they might know me. Hell, I'm no hermit, Felix."

"Well sure, I didn't think you were, Eddy."

"Yeah, that's right. I hit the high spots every now and then. You mean that?"

"No."

"Okay, so what's this 'they' that might know me?"

"Well, grifters maybe.

"Grifters? How do I come to grifters?"

"Hoods."

"Hoods yet," Fleisher said disgustedly. "Listen, pal. I haven't been on that end of the take in a hog's age. Five, maybe six years, right? I'm management now, kid."

Berger grinned. "The big time."

Fleisher grinned back. "Like you said, it's a living."

"Anyway, you used to work out of Philly—in the old days."

"Sure, Philly. That's right."

"Had your own shop."

"For a while. What're you gettin' at?"

"Well, you did mostly local jobs."

"It was a small agency, Felix."

"That's right. Sure. So your mug's no standout in this town?"

"No, I guess not."

Berger nodded. "Okay then."

Eddy Fleisher waved a hand. "I hope you're not going to tell me what this is all about, Felix, and spoil it. Now that I'm used to the merry-go-round, I've grown to like it."

"Hold your horses," Berger said.

"No kidding, I'm enjoying it. I even like the way you came through that window. That showed class."

Berger looked gloomy. "Take it from me, Eddy, you wouldn't want me walkin' in your front door, like I said on the phone."

"Sorry to hear that, son."

"Well, yeah, it could be worse. What about the help in all these plants. Kraft's watchdogs—can they rank you?"

"They wouldn't know me from Adam. What is this? You in some sort of a jam?"

"You could say that."

"The law?"

"Uh-uh."

"Don't tell me," Eddy Fleisher said. "Keep me guessing."

"Remember Bernie?"

"Bernie? A scrawny little bozo. Did odd jobs for you . . ."

Berger sighed, held up his empty glass. "Got another of these?"

Fleisher gave him a refill. Berger took a swig, shuddered slightly and said, "Add Joe Smiley."

"Uh-huh. We were on Bernie."

"Same thing. Know Chuck Foster?"

"Sounds familiar."

"Yeah. Time to time they all hitched a ride on my payroll."

"So what about it?"

Berger said, "They're gone."

"Gone?"

"I had them out on a job, Eddy."

Fleisher looked at him. "You mean rubbed out?"

He shrugged one shoulder, not looking too pleased. "Damn if I know, Eddy. They're just gone."

"What kind of a job?"

"You ain't gonna believe this."

"Try me."

"You know DeKeepa." It was a statement, not a question.

Eddy Fleisher nodded. "Like a rotten tooth," he said.

"That's DeKeepa all right," Berger said. "Now get this: I was hired to spy on DeKeepa spyin' on United Tool."

"That's one of ours from the start. Kraft's got the security angle all sewed up."

"United Tool," Berger said.

Fleisher laughed. "That's slick, all right; that's really something."

"What's so funny?"

"Hell, kid, there's nothing out at that dump."

"Yeah," Berger said gloomily. "Tell that to the boys—next time you see 'em around."

"Maybe," Fleisher said, "they hit it lucky at the track and just took off."

"Sure. All three of 'em. Together. Foster left a wife and six kids."

"That should be reason enough."

"Ho-ho. You're a regular card, Eddy; you ought to send that to Will Rogers. Look, Eddy, Bernie had half a grand comin' to him; you think he'd walk out on that kind of dough? And Smiley just ordered himself a new rig, an Essex. Smiley wouldn't've put down the scratch on that buggy if he was figgering on a fade, would he?"

"I guess not, Felix."

"You're damn right he wouldn't."

"Only it'd still take more'n that to get you crawling through windows, kid."

Berger nodded glumly. "There's more. And it's just as screwy."

"Okay. Let's have it."

"Smiley carried these notebooks, see? Two-by-three dimestore items. Only the covers are alligator hide—the real McCoy, and dyed white. He had them made up special, see?"

"I get the picture."

"Yeah. This Smiley was some Smiley. Well, these books are hard to miss. Like they stand out—"

Eddy Fleisher said, "He used them for what?"

"Well, luck mostly."

"He should get his money back."

"It's this job, Eddy; it don't hang together right; somehow we got stuck on this one. Anyway, Smiley did more'n just lug those things around; he'd jot down his finds, write up the reports from the books."

"And the books went with Smiley?" Fleisher said.

"Yeah," Berger said, "the books went with Smiley."

"Figure he got something solid, huh?"

"That's the size of it."

"And got blotted out for his trouble."

"Yeah."

"Too bad," Eddy Fleisher said. "Any idea what it was?"

"No."

"So it's a bust."

"Maybe not. The book's turned up again, Eddy. At United Tool."

Fleisher smiled. "You're kidding."

"Uh-uh."

"Jesus," he said. "That's screwy, all right."

"Yeah, it sure is."

Fleisher shook his head, pulled at an ear lobe.

Berger said, "In a VP's safe. As pretty as you please."

"This VP got a handle?" Fleisher asked.

"Boris Goren."

"Uh-huh."

"Know him?"

"I know him."

"And?"

"Well, I don't know, Felix; this Goren's always seemed like a harmless enough duffer to me."

"But you don't know."

"No, I don't, but he's always seemed on the up-and-up. How'd you come by all this?"

"I planted a couple of the boys in the joint."

"They still kicking around?"

"Yeah. Last I heard."

"Well, that's something. You want me to get those books for you, is that it?"

"Yeah. That's what I kind of had in mind."

"Okay," Fleisher said. "Sure. Why not?"

"It won't be a cinch," Berger said.

"Leave that to me."

"Goren don't have them no more," Berger said.

"Who does?"

"Earl Kneely."

"Who?"

"He's an accountant at the plant."

"Hell, how does he come into it?"

"He's been nicking them plenty; he seems to've copped the books along with everything else that's caught his eye."

Fleisher laughed. "That's sure some sweet mess you cooked up there, brother."

Berger looked injured. "I got roped into it."

"So this Kneely's beat you out of the books."

"That's what I'm telling you."

"Okay. Anyone besides your boy tumble to it?"

"Uh-uh."

"You sure?"

"Sure, I'm sure."

"Okay. You want me to get in with this Kneely and put the glom on the books—that's what you're peddling, you cagy bastard, isn't it?"

Berger grinned. "Look," he said, "strong arm is out. Like, what if he don't come across? Sure, we can peel his hide off, we can even cut his heart out, right? But what does it get us? We need those damn books. He don't even know what he's got there. How could he? But if he got wise they meant something, we'd never get our mitts on 'em."

"You sure they mean something?"

"I'm not sure of anything."

"That's swell."

"Listen, Eddy, there's something there. Three of the boys are missing and this Goren winds up with the books. I want to take a gander at those books. You blame me?"

"I guess not."

"Listen. We've kept tabs on Kneely. He ain't unloaded most of that stuff yet. That's a fact. This Kneely's a punk, a two-bit crumb. He connects with this fence in the Bronx, see? Maybe later he'll let loose with the rest of the haul. He's bound to comb those books plenty, and if he don't come up with something he can use, that's that. So we got to hustle on this. Let's say we shoot our yap off about this fence and get him collared; that puts him out of circulation, right? Now you step in."

"Me, huh? How do I do that little thing—just waltz on over?"

"Listen. Kneely's thick with this scratch-house bum, this Tom Lacy. That's your in, Eddy. You stand Lacy a round and you own him for life."

"That simple, huh?"

"That simple. You fence the swag, give Kneely a better break than he could get at some other shop. Then, Eddy, you get him to take you to the stash and turn up those books."

"Nothing to it, huh?" Fleisher said. "Who's bankrolling this wild spree?"

"Our client."

"Like that, huh?"

"Like that. I'm cutting you in."

"Thanks, pal. This kind of woozy mess is just what I need to shake up my life."

"There's gold here, Eddy; I wouldn't give you a bum steer."

"Yeah, sure you wouldn't."

"How'd fifty G's sit with you?"

Eddy Fleisher whistled. "That's a lot of boodle, kid."

"There's more'n that around."

"So together," Fleisher said, "we'd be pulling a cool hundred grand."

Berger relit his cigar; his hand shook a little. "More than that, maybe."

"Yeah," Fleisher said, "I think I could go for that, Felix. I think I might get to like that."

"Our client," Berger said, "is rolling in the stuff."

"What's his angle?"

"Well, that's the tough part, all right." Berger looked uncomfortable.

"Spill it," Fleisher said.

"Well, Eddy . . . our client . . . you know . . . says he's in the know about a caper—see?—to knock off everyone from . . . er . . . the President on down."

After a while Eddy Fleisher stopped laughing, got a hanky out and blew his nose. He sat there grinning at Berger like an ape with a boatload of bananas. "You buy that?" he finally asked.

"A hundred grand worth."

"Hell, that's a wooly yarn, all right, Berger. And United Tool's behind it yet."

"Someone at United Tool."

"And what's DeKeepa's dodge?"

"He's a bum. Our client thinks DeKeepa's bunch is sure to tip its mitt and stir up the wolves, maybe make 'em move against DeKeepa."

"The wolves at United? That's some wolves."

"They're the only ones we got."

"Yeah. While you and your boys look on from the shadows."

"Something like that."

"A fishing trip."

"I know," Berger said, "only we've run into something, all right. Look, someone took a shot at me a couple days ago."

"It's probably DeKeepa grousing over playing stooge."

"Don't kid, Eddy; this is damn serious."

"What else do I gotta do besides string this Kneely?"

"Get a line on the United bunch. You got the run of the place. Tell Kraft you're on to something. Think he'll let you scout around?"

"Sure. I can set it up."

"Will you?"

"Is that the crop?"

"Yeah."

"That's not much."

"It's enough."

Eddy Fleisher said, "You really mean it about that fifty grand?"

"I'll write you out a check. Twenty-five now, the rest if you crack Kneely."

"It doesn't matter what's in the books?"

"It doesn't matter."

"Okay. Write me a check."

He wrote it. "Tell me," Berger said. "How do you aim to bust Kneely. You got any notions in that noodle of yours?"

"A couple, kid. Maybe I'll just blow the whistle on him and then get him out of the hole. He'll be grateful."

"He would at that," Berger said.

"What about you, now?"

"I go back out the window."

"Going to duck?"

"For a while. The boys'll keep snooping."

"How do I reach you?"

He shrugged.

"That's nice."

"Try the office first. Or get me at home—"

"That's if the heat's off, eh?"

"Yeah. If the heat's off."

"What if it's not?"

"Try Benny Moon."

"That grifter?"

"Benny's okay. You try him."

"Yeah. Watch your step, kid."

"I'll make out."

"Who's our client, Felix?"

"A guy named James Norton."

"Norton, huh?" Eddy Fleisher shrugged. "I never heard of him."

NORTON FIVE

THE ESTATE

Dr. Corpious bowed.

I had found my way to his lodgings. In one piece. An accomplishment.

Obese. Pop-eyed. Two rows of even white teeth flashed in a black beard. If anyone could help me it would be this man, who knew the city like no one else. Corpious ran the biggest gang of outlaws, of looters, the city had ever seen. Discontent had filled his ranks; paid spies in the Annys kept him informed of any moves against him. But his old friends knew where to find him. And I was one of the oldest.

"I am honored," the fat man's voice boomed.

Old three- and four-story buildings visible through half-drawn curtains. Five blocks of free territory squeezed between Federation blue and Alliance green. The Father Pen estate rose like a beacon in the distance over the East River. A metal wall surrounded the complex. Sentries standing watch.

Dr. Corpious rubbed his hands together. "Loot," he said delightedly. "What a magnificent time for plunder."

I said, "You haven't changed much, I see. Still the same old crook."

"Why not? The city crumbles," he laughed. "It's the game that counts. If I'd changed, Norton, you'd have no use for me. You want a favor, of course."

"How are you doing, Corpious?"

"Far more profitably than the Annys. Flimflammery pays. I spit on the Annys. Grief and gladness mingle in me at this vast opportunity. We'll go the slam, lad!"

"Look," I said, "go easy on that stuff."

Corpious appeared baffled. "But a man must believe in something." He roared with laughter. "May I get you a drink?"

"Better not."

"You're on lift-o then?"

I nodded tiredly.

The fat man's laughter shook the room. He was an irrespressible blob of jelly.

I got down to business. "You remember Nina?"

"Your sister."

"Yes."

"What is the difficulty?"

"She's gone."

"She's run the net?"

"I don't know."

"Time?"

"Three days ago."

He shook his head. "Like chasing the whirly-go, trying to pin her now. It's a shambles out there. Laughter and tears grapple for sovereignty."

"I need your help."

The fat man rose, began to pace the small room. Light danced across his round face like vagrant butterflies. Gunfire could be heard coming from the blue zone, as if a belated festival were getting under way. I stared through the window. In ten minutes I'd seen no one go by.

Corpious said, "These last three days, you've been looking for her?"

"No."

Corpious' eyes sparkled. "You have been away then?"

"That's right."

The fat man sighed. "Who would have suspected it?"

"Suspected *what?*"

"You, Norton. I know about the Cope-Con, you see. You're a Cope. A heretic."

"That's done with."

The fat man raised an eyebrow. "Your sister—"

"I don't know. She's not at the manor, not at work. She may be at Pen's. Don't ask me why."

Corpious sat down heavily. "You don't want much," he said, "do you?"

I shrugged. "I can't get in there."

"Of course; they've posted you."

"I think so. There's more. My partner Brent is gone."

"Yes, I remember him; do you think he and your sister—?"

"You've got it wrong," I said. "They wouldn't have to sneak off to do that."

"You Leaguers," Corpious said. "Your objective, then?"

"In to Pen's."

"That's going the whirl, all right," Corpious said. "But we'll try it. After all—why not?"

Jason Corpious had been one of my most brilliant students at the League academy; that's how we'd become friends. I was glad to see he wasn't taking any of my teachings seriously.

The tunnel went down. Four of us moved along it. One, a small pasty-faced glink, spoke.

"This'll raise the hoots," he said.

Dr. Corpious said, "Be still, Verrik." The tunnel echoed him.

Verrik said, "They'll be eyeing for sure. What we oughtta do, boss, is scratch it. This is just upping the go on our getting downed."

"NO!" Corpious thundered imperiously. That was that.

Light from his pocket-bulb made wings of the shadows that flocked on the walls, set them flapping like bats into frantic motion.

The fourth member of our party—Nord—was at least a head taller than the rest of us, a hulking glink with broad, flat features. So far he had said nothing.

Corpious put a fleshy hand on my shoulder, said, "This is one of the tunnels used by the utility companies. Long ago, when the city functioned as a whole, if such a bizarre concept is still imaginable, these tunnels criss-crossed the entire city—an underground highway. Simply invaluable for those engaged in our somewhat precarious profession. A veritable godsend. Aided me many a time to cup the sweets, slip the loop. Here, away from the intolerable congestion of the upper reaches, a man can find peace, can stroll in meditative contemplation. Notice the scarcity of stop signs, of vehicles. In fact, there are none. A veritable paradise, Norton. Yet totally overlooked by the rabble. And with parks in such scarcity. I cannot bring to mind one park in the city proper, as a matter of fact; can you, Norton?"

I couldn't and said so.

"Precisely. I'd call it a crime, I surely would. Well, the fact is that all regions of the city are accessible from these underground caverns. I've gone, I might add, to the considerable effort and expense of charting them. I can't tell you what a help they've been. Why, right now, when all sorts of unpleasant things are occurring aboveground, we are here below, snug as a bug. And soon we shall be directly *under* the Pen estate. In a matter of minutes . . . if not less."

We crawled up through a hall into a basement.

The Pen estate, a center of commerce. A major sub-cult. Inside its walls strangers would predominate, wouldn't rate a second glance.

"We'll meet here in three hours. It's better to go the way we came," Dr. Corpious said. "Does that give you enough time?"

I said it did.

"Try not to get caught," the pasty-faced Verrik said. "It would give us all a bad name."

"We wouldn't like that," Nord rumbled for the first time.

"I wouldn't care for it much myself," I admitted.

"We're all friends here," Dr. Corpious beamed. "Three hours then."

They turned to go.

I said, "How do I get out of this place?"

They told me. And left.

Following instructions, I made my way to a staircase, then to a chute. No one observed the first leg of my journey; I had plenty of company on the second. But by then it didn't matter; I was one of the annys. The chute doors opened on a streaming street scene: a city in a city of cities. I stepped out into the throng. I wasn't feeling all that dog-eared anymore. I'd cracked the estate.

A hubbub:

It was worse, more congested, in here than on most city walks. Traffic stood still. Walks were a living jam. From the high-walks you could see the East River. What had once been 42nd Street, but was now the Pen-Hikery, cut through the estate like a giant marker.

Some sectors had to be ducked. Checkpoints where seeing-eyes swept over the walks. Ten points in all. I knew where each was. Everyone from mid-echelon up knew.

No signs of the outside conflict here. I stopped to listen for gunshots. In fact, with all the ruckus the traffic made, I couldn't have heard my neighbor if he'd spoken to me. Not that I had that many neighbors left. The glink rubbing elbows with me was probably a potential informer. A shagger. Everyone I touched was a danger to me.

I moved out into the stream. Brothers, fathers, mothers, sisters swept by—prime cultists who lived in, shared the estate with Pen and his phalanx of administrators. Walks bustled with tradesmen, shoppers, high-lifers. I'd been here before, a card-carrying Incest; I'd attended the con-fabs, had twice been a delegate to the All-Incest Congress. But now I felt as out of place as a worm at a trout convention.

Flashing signs boosted incest, extolling it. Loudspeakers murmured the latest incest ditty. The voice-over rambled on, praising Incest leadership—the committee of ten, and most of all, the sublime figure of Father Pen. As though he needed it. The Father's post was hereditary; he was fixed for life; and when he went under, his offspring would carry on.

What were they up to now, I wondered, the committee of ten?

And Father Pen? At this moment of maximum danger to them and their system. Nothing, I'd wager. They were notoriously irresponsible, as loopy as an alley cat loose in a catnip dispensary.

Finding Nina in this crush was a job for wardens. But I could suppose a few possibilities: she'd come here either on business or pleasure.

The matron at the Orgy Temple said, "We get hundreds here, all the high-lifers. Can't keep track. Never could."

So much for pleasure.

Nina was a flacker in the League Public Confidence office, which had close ties to the Cult Public Confidence office. I tried it. They knew us both, but hadn't seen the girl recently. So much for business.

There were always friends.

Miss Henrietta Johnson ran an apparel den on the main strip.

"Why no," she said, "why?"

"I thought she might have been here."

Henrietta Johnson shrugged. "It's always a pleasure to see dear Nina, but I can't claim the privilege this week."

I made my excuses and went away.

There were lots of places I could visit, and during the next hour I visited a good many of them:

Brother Shade shook his bewhiskered head. "No," he said emphatically. "Have you tried Barbara?"

"Yes," Sister Shade said sympathetically, "why don't you do that?"

Barbara didn't know what I was talking about. "Not for *two months*," she said indignantly. I had hit, it seemed, an ex-friend.

"Hardly," Brother Moore told me.

"I can't imagine," Brother Clayton said.

Stopping under a high-walk, I decided to make myself ridiculous. Holding the marble in my palm, I addressed it earnestly and passionately. I had lost faith in the bubble, I couldn't deny that, and the lack of response I now received did nothing to restore it.

I rejoined the crowds and wondered if I ought to go on with my list of friends, acquaintances, and business connections. It seemed a waste, but what else could I do?

I knew of some Copes lowing it in the estate, but with this raid-week in full swing I wouldn't feel safe within a mile of them; any-way, Nina hardly knew them.

A think-board caught my eye, at estate center. Conventions, semi-nars, special classes. A small group of historians from five Annys had been holding a session for almost a week. Brent had said something about turning up there. I still had two hours before my rendezvous with Corpious. None of my other visits had started alarms clinging: things were too muddled to make for good communication and my fall from grace was still a buried fact. So why not mingle with my fellow colleagues? I took down the hall number and headed in that direction.

It was about time I did something smart.

No problem getting into the place. I rode up a moving-walk to level two. A mini-social in progress. I couldn't have timed it any bet-ter. I joined them.

Faces turned in greeting—smiling, friendly faces. I drifted from group to group. These Annys knew who I was. They didn't know what I had become. It didn't seem too likely that they would find out during the next few minutes. I started asking about Brent.

"Oh yes," George Blake said, blinking myopically in my direction. "Here somewhere, you know."

I hadn't known—it seemed too easy; and Brent was nowhere in sight. Two more elderly scholars attested to seeing him.

Through the crowd I spied Thomas Pratt. I made my way to him, put a hand on his elbow. Pratt turned a startled face toward me, disengaged himself from a cluster of chattering professors. Together we pushed our way to a small island of relative calm behind a mar-ble pillar.

Thomas Pratt was a Cope.

Artificial green leaves climbed out of an imitation vase to our right. A bare wall was our backdrop. I hoped there were no bugs.

I hadn't seen Pratt at the Cope-Con and asked him about it. "Passed it up," Pratt said. "Let them go one without me. Seem to have sat out the finale, though. What did they get on us?"

"Everything."

"They catch Weber?"

Weber. The man in the black mask. The founder of the Copes. I had almost forgotten about him. His day had come and gone. "I don't know," I said.

Pratt looked tired. A short, rumpled man at the end of his rope.

I said, "What are you doing here, Pratt?"

"Having a last fling, it seems. You were in the city?"

"I passed through."

"Well?"

"What do you expect?" I said.

"There is an irresistible desire on my part, you see, to wait and observe exactly what happens."

"Forget it, Pratt. Get out while you can."

"Get out?"

"The hills, perhaps."

Pratt looked at me. "I've heard nothing."

"Colonies."

"A fact?"

"A rumor."

"Personally, Norton, I'd rather not be the one to check it out."

A small bent figure approached us. "Gentlemen," it said, grinning at us out of a seamed, elderly face, "in times such as these, it gives one courage to know that so fine and upright an Anny as the Alliance exists for those who are troubled by confusion . . . so to speak . . . a lighthouse in the wilderness . . ."

I said, "We're Leaguers," making my voice stern.

"It's never too late," the elderly party said cheerfully. "Think up." He winked and shambled off.

"Pratt," I said, "you seen anything of Brent?"

"He was here."

"Was?"

"Gone now. Didn't notice when. Not with all this excitement."

"Excitement?" I looked around. It was as lively as a high-school tea.

"Scholars, you know," Pratt said. "I meant out there. The sad truth has penetrated even to this sector of unreality. These walls will be next to go."

"How does three days ago sound?"

"For Brent?" He thought it over. "About right, I'd guess."

"And now?"

"He could be anywhere," Pratt said.

"But not here?"

"Definitely not here. Funny, everyone seems to be looking for Brent. Some men were asking about him."

"Who?"

"They didn't say. But they seemed to mean business."

"Security?"

"That was the general impression. Only by then your friend had already gone. Yes, Brent has really become quite popular. Your Nina was asking for him too."

That stopped me. "Nina?"

"After he had left. And before the others came."

"Details," I said.

"She left almost at once. Charming girl. Seemed most anxious. That's all there is."

"Did she say what she wanted?"

"Only Brent."

"Did she say where she was going?"

"Not to me. She had her head together with Lorry. Lorry's here somewhere."

We went to find Lorry.

"Ah, yes," Lorry said, excusing herself from two male admirers. She was a stunning brunette who wore dark glasses. "Brent," she said, "was looking for Schluss."

"Schluss?" I said.

"Yes. He was most insistent."

Schluss was a junior-grade League administrator. As far as I knew, Schluss and Brent had never been that close.

"And did he find Schluss?" I said.

"Not here," she said. "But I sent him along to the right place. The Other-Worlders."

"He's an Other-Worlder?" Pratt said.

"Always has been," Lorry said.

"When did this happen?"

"Three days ago."

"You exchanged some words with Nina. What did you tell her?"

"What I've just told you. All about Brent and Schluss. About six hours after Brent's departure. Just what is this?—if you're telling, of course."

"They seem to have become missing."

"Both? There's a war going on out there."

"Did you tell any of this to security?"

"Not this girl."

"You're an angel," I said.

Outside, I had two choices: wait for Corpious or take a walk on my own. If I went through the gates, I'd make it out all right—up to a point—but once on the outside the scanners would probably spot me and it would be touch and go. Not an enviable position. The underground route was safest, but that would mean another hour and a half waiting for the good doctor and his companions.

One way to remain out of sight was to crawl off to the dark hole in the sub-basement. But in the unlikely event that Corpious attracted a crowd, I'd be bottled in. Taking off alone in the underground tunnels didn't appeal to me either. It would be like running a maze. If I found my way out—and that was a big if—it would probably be in the wrong place, like, say, under the stockade.

I moved along the walk, letting the alternatives jog around my brain.

Events got in the way of any easy decisions I might reach.

Sirens began to rise and quiver, as if a truckload of dragons were being molested. I and just about everyone else stopped to listen. Were we under siege?

A familiar figure appeared on an upper ramp, running. The crowd bounced away as if a stream of lava had been loosed on it. For a man his size, Nord could certainly run. His footwork was impressive. The laser in his large fist wasn't really necessary—the look of desperation on his giant's face was enough. I was glad he was on that upper ramp; the farther away the better. I saw no sign of Dr. Corpious or Verrik. I didn't spend much time worrying about it.

Then Nord was gone. Out of sight. Other things were in sight, even less pleasant. Wardens were springing up like toadstools. The sirens were still screeching like a band of throttled apes.

Pedestrians, fickle as always, were beginning to desert the walks; traffic had slowed up.

I knew what would happen next. Walks emptying out, manors filing up. By tens and twenties the Annys would be herded into rooms and auditoriums. Each would be given a thorough spot-check.

No one would be going in or out of the estate gates now. I could only go one way—down.

Three manors to my left, four to my right, with ramps running off at different angles. I was on the middle one. Narrow spikes connected buildings and ramp.

I moved toward the only structure that would do me any good, the tallest of the lot—the Hall of Justice, security police headquarters. Not the best place for a posted glink, but the only manor within trotting distance with a lower-level walk. If I hoped to jump the clutch, to leave the estate under my own steam, it would have to be through the underground maze. That was certain now. To get to that hole in the ground I'd have to go as far down as possible, and that meant through the Justice building.

No one took much notice of me inside. I could see why. The place was in an uproar. It must have been years since bells had clamored and chimed in the estate itself. So much for the impregnable fortress theory. Everything was pregnable these days—including me. It was the spirit of the age.

A man ran up too me, one in civvies.

"What's going on, for Pen's-sake?" he wailed.

"Attack!" I bellowed over the racket.

The man ran away.

A group of armed wardens sprinted past me on the double. Heads stuck out of office doors, jabbering at one another.

A long marble corridor took me away from men and commotion. Soon I would be in the building's center.

And the chutes.

A flick of a button and I'd be heading down. It'd be hard without

Corpious as guide, but I'd manage. Somewhere along the line I'd pick up Nina and Brent. The three of us would head out for points unknown. What was left of the system would hardly miss us.

A chute was waiting. The noise was now a distant, insignificant rumble. It had nothing to do with me anymore. Stepping into the chute's cool and polished interior, I punched the down button.

The doors swung shut, clicking into place.

A magnified voice vibrated in the small enclosure. "James Norton," it said, "you have been a grave disappointment to us all. Await your punishment, James Norton. It will be swift and final, as it must be, but no less than you deserve—James Norton, sinner."

I recognized the voice.

It was Father Pen.

Then the chute began racing up.

The doors opened on a medium-sized room. I didn't go out at once. I did things to the chute buttons and listened to them click. Nothing doing.

Then I went into the room.

The chute doors slammed behind me. The mechanism sprang to life, whirled off in its shaft.

I looked around. I was in a padded cell. No furniture of any kind. No door, even. The thinnest crack in the padding showed where the chute had been. Three walls were padding, the fourth opaque glass. Someone had erred. I could now bash my brains out against the glass. But I wasn't ready for that just yet.

I looked at the glass, knowing what it was, and as if in response an image appeared on it and looked back at me.

The round face. The tufts of white hair. The full lips and bulbous nose. I was standing eyeball to eyeball with Father Pen himself. The image spoke.

"Shame on you," it said. "Good Norton, is this how you repay your friends? A Cope, good Norton! The dagger thrust in the very back of your Anny, the worthy League, and the womb itself which nurtured you, Incest—home of your brothers and sisters. How, good Norton, could you do us so great a wrong?"

I started an answer—I had a lot of them—but the question was only rhetorical. The voice rode over me, drove on:

"We who have seen you through our nurseries, through our grade schools, and into our institutes of higher learning—were we not there, good Norton, when you needed us most? Did we not supply you"—and here the fat lips paused to smack against one another—"with an *ideal* partner to remain at your side as you journeyed through life, and blessed the match with the official sanction of our all-powerful Cult? It was bliss, good Norton, that you had—boundless, bountiful bliss. What more could we render you on this mortal coil? Yet there are still ways to make amends; you can cleanse your sullied conscience, redress at least part of the wrongs you have done us, done yourself, by making a clean breast of things. Get it off your chest, good Norton."

That's all I needed. A mind-cleansing at the good Father's expense. Before the coup de grace.

I had one question:

"How'd you find me, Pen? I thought I was doing pretty well."

The fat face stared at me.

"Why, Jimmy," it said, "you ought to know. The Hall of Justice is honey-combed with spotter eyes. The computer singled you out at once. It was a foolish move on your part, Jimmy, to breach the spider's web. Whatever possessed you, Jimmy, to do such a thing? And a Cope, yet?"

I said, "You think you'll survive this upheaval, retain your palace, your precious status?" But he was right. I'd blundered terribly. Too much pressure on me perhaps; one lift-o too many. *Mind-dysfunction.* My memory had sprung a fatal leak.

"A minor disturbance," Pen replied. "A mere incident. The fools don't know when they're well off."

"The fools," I said, "seem to be taking over."

"We have means of coping with the herd; that should come as no surprise to you, Jimmy. You must have learned something as League historian. No, Jimmy. There is a staying power to the Cult. The Annys themselves are perhaps fragile, a thing of the moment. Many of the old Annys—those that pioneered our system, that sat it on its feet in the old, dark days of chaos and disorder—are now no more.

Bowed out. Mere names in the history books—were history books still a fashionable commodity. But then you know all that. In the Archives the records still exist. I am certain you have not overlooked them. Gone, gone those old cherished names NAM, AMA, A&P . . . They were inordinately fond of initials, those people, eh? But they had the right idea, Jimmy: self-interest. What could be simpler, more direct? Some, alas, fell by the wayside, the victims of internal contradictions or of forces quite beyond their control. Crumbled, and other amalgamous conglomerates rose to take their place—figuratively speaking, of course. What Anny could truly take the place of another? Why, they're unique! But perishable. That, Jimmy, is my point. The Incest Cult does not perish. It endures. It survives. It shall—in its own manner, no doubt—continue to do so. Where others fall by the wayside, it strides on. And why not? Our Cult provides a needed service. Whereas—and this is quite between us, Jimmy—some Annys (and they shall remain nameless) provide only the rudiments of service, the bare trappings. Small wonder they decline. But by studiously avoiding identification with any single Anny, by allying ourselves, as it were, with a wide spectrum of Annys, we have managed, quite magnificently, to flourish. What we offer, of course, is sanctioned transgression. And if the common Annys look in abhorrence at our ways, the greater our profit! We offer the realization of the ultimate forbidden desire. What could be more tantalizing? More enticing? Why, Jimmy—don't you see?— what we have here is a going concern. The disorder you speak of might better be termed a slight readjustment. There have been many such adjustments through the years, but your presence here, the fact that you *are*, attests to the inherent stability of our order. Wouldn't you say?"

"No," I said, "not necessarily. Actually, there are a number of possibilities. One of them being that your number's finally come up."

The Incest Cult had been around almost from the start. Since the Nazi-Soviets won the war and lost the peace. Upheavals came. The first blight lasting for over a decade as the winning powers struggled among themselves and the system fell to bits. State power went down. And the Annys and cults took over. And incest thrived from the word go.

"Is that why you left us, Jimmy? You fear we're passé?"

"Your palace is built on a junk heap," I said. "Aside from being a pretty rickety proposition, it's kind of hard on the junk."

"You fret for the riff-raff? The junk, Jimmy, will have to look after itself."

"I suppose that goes for me too."

"You have placed yourself outside my protection. It is a condition, Jimmy, that has a certain permanency about it. Still, it was nice having this chat."

The screen went blank.

So far no one had bothered to drop around in person. I was still armed to the teeth. That is, I had my laser. I took it out now and ran my eyes over the chamber. I was looking for a target. I didn't find any. I decided not to let that stand in my way.

I turned the gun on the screen and there was a sound like eggs frying. A webwork of fine cracks appeared in the glass. That was all. I'd knocked out their viewer, but I hadn't helped myself any. Negative progress. There wasn't much point in just damaging their property. What I needed was an exit. Again I pulled the trigger. The egg-frying session was over, it seemed. I'd already done my worst. Nothing else happened to the screen. That told me something. The place was probably tamper-proof. The room had a special purpose. I didn't know exactly what that might be, but I was beginning to guess. I didn't like what I guessed. I worked over the padding with the laser beam. It smoldered, burst into flames. Flames danced over the wall. The room began to fill with smoke. But the fire wasn't making much headway: the fabric—whatever it was—must have been chemically treated. I wasn't going to roast just yet. The smoke would get me first. I was going to suffocate. I had tried my best—if it could be called that—and it hadn't been good enough. That's what it came down to. I was about to pay the price.

I got as far away from the smoke as possible—which wasn't very far—crouched in a corner and looked around desperately. The flames were spreading slowly. They wouldn't get me. The smoke was growing denser. *That* would get me.

A voice from my pocket said, "If you remain here, the smoke will surely get you."

If I'd had any false teeth, I'd have dropped them. It was lucky my nose didn't fall off.

"I'd already figured that out," I told the bubble.

"I can't seem to leave you alone for an instant without something dire occurring," the bubble said.

"Instant?" I coughed.

"Even bubbles have business to attend to," the bubble observed.

"Come on," I said, "let's quit the repartee and get me out of here before something bad happens."

"Something bad *is* happening. You see? I warned you. Still, it could be worse."

"How?"

"They haven't released the poison gas yet."

He was right; it could be worse.

"Yes, my dear Norton, what you are in, besides trouble, is a gas chamber."

"So why haven't they gassed me?"

"The fire seems to have put them off a bit. Perhaps they're waiting to see what will happen next."

"So am I. Can they still see me?"

"Assuredly. The screen you fractured was of secondary importance. At this moment you are being monitored by a number of observers, Father Pen not least among them. Your behavior must be a puzzle to them. It would appear that you have quite taken leave of your senses. What they see, my dear Norton, is a man in the last stages of mental decline, one crouching helplessly in a corner and jabbering to himself. Naturally, they can't hear me. The spectacle must fascinate them. So sudden a breakdown. It must make them wonder. That is probably the reason they have withheld the gas. That, and the fact that the gas is no doubt combustible. I'm not sure they know what will happen if the gas makes contact with the fire. In any case, your life or death is really of no great importance to them. Not at this juncture, certainly, with riots and rebellion rife in the city. Under other circumstances, perhaps their interest would be keener. The psychology of the heretic has always been a matter of concern to the Lacers. But for now your state of mind or impending demise is only, at best, a diversion. That, in short, is the situation."

"You've left something out," I said.

"Oh?"

"The most important part."

"I can't imagine what, my dear Norton. I have tried to be most thorough. I feel it is vitally important that we develop rapport, a mutual trust. I want you to have confidence in my abilities—"

"What are we still doing here? *That's* what you've left out. Just look at this mess. In another second I won't be able to see a thing, the smoke's so thick, let alone breathe. What about it?"

"Oh. I see. Well, rest assured, in another second you won't be here."

"I won't? When you say 'rest,' I take it you don't mean eternal?"

"Lying prone as you are now sensibly doing, my dear Norton, will provide you with that extra moment of oxygen we need."

"So it's 'we' again, is it?"

"Notice how the ceiling is quite clouded up."

"I couldn't help noticing."

"Also the wall is becoming quite crisp over there. Fried to a cinder, in fact."

"I noticed that too."

"Well, two things are about to occur, almost simultaneously."

"I give up the ghost and you go back where you came from."

"Such pessimism! The smoke, you see, has risen to the ceiling. It is up there that they have their viewers, which are now, incidentally, almost useless. Already they have lost sight of you in the smoke. Secondly, the wiring in the wall was not meant to withstand a conflagration; it is almost burned through and consequently useless. There is a door amid all that padding, one that alone you could never hope to find. But I can show you."

"You'd better hurry," I pointed out. The room was starting to do peculiar things. It was spinning and contracting. The walls seemed to be slipping down to my shoulders.

There was a popping sound.

"Well," the bubble said. "There you are. Actually, my counsel was hardly needed. You would have done quite well on your own. That, my dear Norton, was the door opening."

"Where?"

"Wires melted," the bubble chuckled. "I *am* really beginning to enjoy this. Just crawl straight ahead."

"I seem to be doing a lot of crawling lately," I gasped.

"The situation calls for it, I'm afraid. You can't blame *me* for *that.*"

My nose banged against the wall.

"Now what?"

"Push it. A little over to your left."

"Like this?"

"Precisely."

"All right," I said. "I'm pushing."

"You'll have to do better than that."

I got off my belly and half-way stood up. This didn't work out the way it was supposed to. The floor seemed to tilt under me. I fell through the door.

"Yes, that's one way of doing it," the bubble said.

Smoke, thick and acrid, poured out of the doorway behind me. I was in a hallway. So far, I was its only occupant. I lay dreamily on the cold floor, trying to catch my breath. It seemed to be a full-time job, and I put a lot of effort into it.

The voice from my pocket said urgently, "The smoke is clearing in there. Any instant they'll become aware of your absence. Push the door closed, Norton. Up on your feet, Norton. If they lay hands on you now, all this will have been wasted. Naught! Naught! Naught! You hear me?"

"To hear is to obey," I sighed.

" 'Tis a wise child," the bubble said.

"You're telling me."

I'd gotten as far as one of the chutes when the personnel began appearing. It wasn't much of a bout, after all. The bubble had spotted the pair of wardens while they were still around the bend. A bad place to be spotted. As they came plodding along, I stepped out from behind a pillar and clobbered them both to the floor. I used the gun. My bare hands were too busy shaking to be much good at infighting.

This, I knew, was the time to do something especially clever. Nothing occurred to me. I settled on the obvious. A warden's cloak went around my shoulders. Buttoned, it reached close to my ankles. An instant warden. Better than donning the whole costume, too. This way I could switch roles as the situation demanded. I helped myself to a stun gun. The laser is a peerless weapon, but there's no way to use it without doing permanent damage. The stunner might save me from murder.

A chute rocketed me down to basement one. Another to the subbasement. Something started to clang just about then, but it was a long way off—upstairs. The management had finally caught on. I imagined the doors and windows snapping shut in that old, futile exercise that these glinks so love to indulge in. I had popped another lift-o into my mouth and was ready to take on the world again. By tomorrow it would probably kill me. But tomorrow seemed a long way off. Unreachable, in fact.

Ten minutes later I was back at the hole. It was a lonely place now, and I didn't waste any time mooning over lost company.

"You can see me through the maze?" I asked conversationally.

The bubble chuckled. There was a contemptuous note to the sound.

That was good enough for me.

FLEISHER FIVE

KRAFT

It was still raining Wednesday morning. A little shy of 11 A.M.

Eddy Fleisher put on a fresh shirt, wound a collar around his neck, tied a knot in a polka-dot tie. Trousers were powder blue and fashionably wide; the jacket was gray-blue, double-breasted, wide-lapeled, with just the right roll of padding in the shoulders. A long, belted raincoat and soft-brimmed hat rounded out his attire. He was ready. He put a gun in a hip holster, shoved his wallet in a pocket, picked up an umbrella and a black satchel full of yesterday's loot, and went off to his favorite eatery.

Vitali's was a smoky chophouse over on Lex. At this in-between hour, Eddy Fleisher had the place virtually to himself. Taking a table by the window, he watched the rain as it made narrow rills down the pane; people and umbrellas moved along swiftly outside. Eddy Fleisher killed a double orange juice, a plate of bacon and eggs, some rolls and coffee, while he ran his eyes over the *Times'* front page:

ROOSEVELT IS COLD TO BONUS. A *chilly word for the working stiff—as usual.*

HUGE BUYING WAVE IS HELD IMMINENT . . . BUSINESS ACTIVITY WILL IMPROVE . . . *Some rubes will swallow just about anything . . .*

Mayor LaGuardia, it said, was saying something or other. *The job called for it.*

Page Two read:

NEW RELIEF PLAN DUE HERE JULY 15. *One in a long*

line of plans. This one promised relief for women, too. That was a change. But would it bring happiness and real deep-down contentment? Would anything?

Fleisher turned his attention to the important news in the back pages:

ROAMING BEAR BAGGED IN PARK ZOO.

BRONX GREETS UNLOVELY AARD-VARK.

EDDIE CANTOR IN HOSPITAL. MINOR STOMACH AILMENT.

LISTERINE SHAVING CREAM. STYPTIC COTTON BATH FOR 25¢ . . .

Thirty-five cents covered the chow. He could remember when it had been twenty-five. He left a nickel tip and went back into the rain.

After a fifteen-minute hike through puddles and midtown traffic, Eddy Fleisher was swapping hellos with the switchboard operator. The decal on the frosted-glass door said KRAFT. Eddy Fleisher found his way to the office he used when in town. The Kraft Agency took up half a floor. Faces had kept changing with each of his visits; turnover was pretty high, but par for the course. As Fleisher came in, the rest of the crew headed out. Lunch hour. It looked as though he'd never get to be one of the boys. He could stand the gaff. It was an ambition he had given up after the age of nine.

His desk, he saw, was piled high with papers. He looked at them. The nabobs of United Tool were screaming bloody murder. They seemed to have developed an instantaneous and weirdly collective persecution complex, imagining themselves watched and spied upon.

Eddy Fleisher sat down in his swivel chair and the phone rang.

"I was transferred to you, Mister Fleisher," a voice said in his ear. The voice didn't sound any too neighborly. "This is an outrage," the voice shouted at once. That made it one of the United bunch; theirs was the only outrage that might concern him.

"You are who?" Eddy Fleisher asked.

"This is Springer."

Springer would be nothing less than chairman of the board.

Eddy Fleisher said, "Yes sir."

"I am told that you have been placed in charge of special security?"

Eddy Fleisher said that was the case.

"But you've done *nothing*."

"That's not true, sir."

"I'm being followed, Fleisher."

"I know."

"You *know?* Then why don't you stop the scoundrels?"

"They're our men."

"What?"

"Our men are covering the plant, sir; we're keeping the board of directors, the chief executives, under surveillance."

Springer thought he knew why. There'd been losses, after all. "Well?! What have you found?"

"A full report," Fleisher said, "will be issued within the coming week, sir."

"Report? What report?" the voice screamed. "I want action, not reports. Action, I say! Action!" The voice had become hoarse. With a lot of effort, Fleisher figured, he would probably understand what it was Springer wanted. It was time to say something positive and Fleisher said it: "Don't worry, we're looking into it." He added that the situation was under control. Probably it was the wrong thing to say.

The voice became ominous:

"Control, you say? Control? Let me tell you something, Mr. Fleisher. Our patience is almost at an end. You hear me, Mr. Fleisher? We've been with Kraft for five years, five long years. You are aware of that, I trust?"

"Yes sir."

"Well, Mr. Fleisher, I wouldn't expect *that* situation to continue much longer. You understand me, Mr. Fleisher?"

Eddy Fleisher said he understood.

"Then kindly convey my sentiments to Mr. Kraft."

He said he would.

The phone slammed down in Eddy Fleisher's ear.

One hell of a note. A few more like that and he'd be hopping a rattler with that grubber Tom Lacy. If this turned out to be a flop, he'd end up on the relief lines himself. It wasn't a prospect he could view with much eagerness.

He sighed. In the black satchel resting near his right foot there was more than enough merchandise to put him on easy street for a good long while. Only he wasn't ready for that kind of a play. Not yet, he wasn't.

The buzzer sounded.

Eddy Fleisher picked up the phone. The receptionist's voice said, "The old man'd like to see you, Eddy."

"Swell, honey."

Hefting his satchel, Eddy Fleisher carted it over to the boss's office.

"What's this," Oswald Kraft said, "about you knocking over United Tool last night?"

Kraft was a medium-sized man of fifty-five or so, with thinning brown hair and a worried frown on his otherwise jovial face. Hazel eyes flicked over Fleisher nervously. "Well?"

Fleisher plunked down the satchel on Kraft's desk. "Here's the haul."

Kraft managed a grin; obviously he didn't want to believe that one of his ops would do anything quite so foolish as stick up a client. Without too great a show of conviction, he said, "The description matches you, Eddy."

"It does, huh?"

"To the letter."

"Well, whaddya know?" Fleisher said, exhibiting some wonder.

"I don't like the way you're taking this," Kraft said suspiciously, his eyes becoming suddenly alert.

Fleisher shrugged, snapped open the satchel. "Rest your peepers on these."

Kraft bent over the desk, took a long, steady look. What he saw was money in all dimensions, securities, bonds, an assortment of confidential memos, some pages copied from United ledgers. Kraft let out his breath, his gaze coming to rest on Fleisher.

Fleisher chuckled. "This score was the nuts. A nice wad, huh, skipper?"

Kraft's fist pounded the desk. "Can it!" he roared. Then: "Er . . . you didn't really heist the tool works, did you, Eddy boy?"

"Nope. Scout's honor, boss."

"But," Kraft said, inclining his head an inch toward the satchel, "you did something."

"Yep."

"Care to tell me what?"

"Sure."

"I'm glad," Kraft said, reaching into a desk drawer. He took out a paper bag, and removing a sandwich from it, commenced eating. "Go on," he said, "tell me. You can trust me, Eddy boy," he said between chews. "I'm just curious how you're going to weasel out of this one, that's all. Just maybe, Eddy boy, this time you've gone a bit too far, eh? I mean, that's a possibility. Or don't you agree? Go ahead, tell me. Sorry I can't offer you any of this," he said, wagging his half-eaten sandwich, "but I wasn't really expecting company for lunch. Go on—tell me."

Fleisher told him: "I didn't boost any of this swag. All I did was spring Earl Kneely."

"So it *was* you, eh?"

"Sure. But I didn't grab off any of this load."

"You didn't?"

"Uh-uh."

"Then, if I might inquire . . . it *is* all right with you, Eddy boy, if I inquire?"

"Sure. It's aces with me, chief."

"Well, that's just dandy. And how did you come by all this hot stuff, Eddy?"

"It's the cat's pajamas, eh, chief?"

"How'd you get it, Fleisher?"

"It was a gift from Kneely for springing him."

"Kneely? Who is Kneely?"

"A bookkeeper at the plant."

"So?"

"Our boys bagged him copping the stuff."

"Ah!"

"That's right. And I dropped around to put him back in circulation."

"Nice of you," Kraft said cheerfully. "And you were rewarded accordingly, I see."

"It was the psychology of the moment, chief. I'd counted on that. He couldn't turn me down. We split three ways."

"Oh. The third man, *your accomplice*, got his too, eh?"

"Sure. Only I wouldn't exactly call him my accomplice, boss."

"Who was he, Fleisher?"

"Tom Lacy. A drifter, strictly a gapper."

"Fine company you keep."

"All part of the hustle."

"Certainly. And besides this prize here, there was, no doubt, *a reason* for freeing this Kneely person."

"He couldn't've stood the pinch and neither could we. It's the god's truth. None of this is fresh haul, Mr. Kraft. We'd've come up with empty hands if we'd collared him on the spot. He's been nicking the joint like clockwork, on a regular basis, and stashing the haul out in the sticks. It was mostly luck that he got away with it this long. I guess we've been slipping up some on that job, all right. This Kneely shows every sign of being strictly a country cousin. I set him up for the fall."

After wiping his hands on a napkin, Kraft produced a bottle of beer from the same desk drawer that had held the sandwich. Popping the cap with an opener he carried on his key chain and taking a healthy swig, Kraft said, "Sorry, I've only got one bottle."

"That's okay," Fleisher said. "I'm not really in the mood anyway."

"That's good," Kraft said, "because I don't have any extra."

"Don't mind me, boss."

"I'm certainly trying not to. Look, Eddy, where'd you get the dope? I mean, how'd you wise up to this bookkeeper . . . ?"

"This is gonna be embarrassing to the whole agency, Mr. Kraft, but you know Felix Berger, don't you?"

"Berger? Our *competition*, you mean?"

"I guess you could say that. Yeah. Anyway, he's an old pal of mine; we were rookie cops in the same precinct maybe ten years back. Felix tipped me."

Kraft raised an eyebrow. "And how did *he* know? Surely it wasn't common knowledge out on the street?"

"Well, no, not exactly. Berger's got a couple of guys in the plant."

"In *our* plant? What the hell are they doing there?"

"That's the screwy part, all right. Berger's on a job. This party who's footing the bill for Felix is a puzzler, an unknown quantity, but loaded—that much is pretty sure. That's about all that *is* pretty sure. This party's got it in his noodle that there's a trick in the works to knock off a crop of big shots and that somehow it's all tied in with the tool works—"

"Who's 'this party'?"

"How's James Norton for a tag?"

Kraft shrugged.

"You ain't the only one. Berger ran a check on him. Routine, right? Well, he drew a blank."

"But he's loaded?"

"Like a barrel. According to Felix, this Norton's got the cabbage growing out of his ears."

"Yet there's no record of him," Kraft mused. "That's a bit unusual, isn't it?"

"It's dizzy. There's more, too. Three of Berger's boys upped and pulled a Crater—they just vanished. One of 'em had a habit of toting around notebooks like these."

He fished in a jacket pocket and brought out the white-skinned alligator notebooks—two of them. Kraft ruffled through the pages.

After a while Kraft said, "I don't get it."

"Neither do I. Full of monikers, dates, that kind of thing—all connected with this job, I guess, only it don't mean anything as far as I can see."

"Where'd it come from, Eddy?"

"Goren's safe. After Berger's op skipped or—more likely—was knocked off, this stuff turned up in Goren's safe. Berger's men spotted it. But before he could do much, Kneely glommed it, along with the more negotiable goods. Probably looked like something to him. He'd been copying ledgers, too. Figuring he could peddle some tool works dope to the competition. Anyway, the books went into a hole with the rest of the goodies. So to get to them, I had to get this dumb-cluck accountant off the hook and then get him to come across with a piece of the loot. I was a stranger to Kneely. I'd been

fencing the stuff—supposedly—and at a whopping profit for him.
Tom Lacy was my mister fix, the go-between. That's one lousy mutt
for you, that Lacy. You should see the way he dogs it in a tight spot.
Anyway, I had our boys cop Kneely and then I cut him loose. And
here you've got the results. Whatever that means—and don't ask me
—I don't know. Incidentally, both Kneely and Lacy picked up a tail
—I set them up—so the rest of the swag is more or less in sight.
With what I've been shelling out for those bonds and things, they're
both bound to turn up for a refill. You can't beat my prices, boss."

"This Norton's bankrolling you?"

"Yeah."

"Well, well," he said.

"Goren's in this somewhere. Berger's been trying to run down our
old pal Grace Waller."

This Waller dame—a United Tool exec—had skipped a while
back. No one could find her.

"Any luck?"

"Uh-uh. But he figures Goren's the key. What do you think?"

"It's a bitcheroo," Kraft said levelly.

"You won't get any argument out of me, skipper. By the way,
Springer just called. He's sore."

"About what?"

"Thinks someone's spying on the whole tool works bunch."

"He's on to Berger?"

"Uh-uh. DeKeepa."

Kraft sighed. "Okay, tell me." Fleisher told him how DeKeepa
fit into it, how DeKeepa had been hired to inadvertently stir things
up. When he had finished, Kraft swore long and loud and with
considerable ability and conviction. "It's a ball-breaker," he finally
said.

Eddy Fleisher admitted it.

"That Springer is poison to tangle with," Kraft said. "And now
you've got the agency all jammed up with him."

"Not me, chief. Norton, Kneely, Berger, and Goren maybe. Grace
Waller maybe. Any of the other boys on the board: Thomson,
Robeson, Canner, Smallwood, Oppenheimer, Ruskin—you name
'em. But not me. I'm a babe in the woods compared to those birds.

I'm a real latecomer—but if you want to know what *I* think, I'll be glad to tell you."

Kraft looked tired. "Why don't you?"

"All this is more than just a lot of hooey."

"Yeah?"

"I'm betting if we put the needle in Goren, he'll crack."

"Goren is somebody."

"He won't be when we're through with him."

"You've got to handle this yourself."

"Okay."

"And if he keeps his clam shut?"

"That's a bad break. He won't, though; I'll feed him a line. Don't worry. I'll put him through the wringer."

"What if he doesn't stand for the shake? Let's say he raises a holler, eh?"

"I'm betting he won't; he's in too deep."

"And if, while you're doing all this, the board starts to squawk, Eddy?"

"Soft-pedal it. Keep it under glass, Mr. Kraft. We can get the kicks squared later."

"If your hunch pans out, Eddy."

"It's more than a hunch."

"There's too damn much riding on this. The Agency can sink—"

"Look. Make it my party. Put the blame on me. Give me a couple of days to work it out. Just sit tight and let me work it out. Goren's ripe for the fall. I can feel it."

"You'd be taking a helluva chance, Eddy."

Fleisher told him, "This whole deal isn't kosher. If we come out on top, it's a feather in our caps. And what's more, there's still a nice buck to be made. I tell you, I wouldn't be doing this for pretzels. There's something big going on." Fleisher didn't bother to explain that he'd already collected twenty-five grand on the deal.

For a moment Kraft was quiet. "All right," he finally said, "take a couple of days."

"Thanks, chief."

"And if you queer it, Eddy?"

"Who gives a hoot? That's my look-out, isn't it? I'm betting I come out on top."

"Let's say you don't?"

Fleisher got to his feet. "Search me," he said. "Better put this stuff in the safe," indicating the satchel. Ducking his head, he went away.

NORTON SIX

THE STOCKADE

There was fighting near the Other-Worlders' Temple. Schluss was in there somewhere. And he knew about Nina and Brent. The walks were blocked off. A question now whether the warden's cloak I had on would be an asset or a liability. I thought it over and voted for liability. The bubble disagreed. "They will respond to authority," it said. "They are, you recall, a sanctioned heresy. They would not wish to jeopardize their standing."

That was true enough.

I looked over the intervening walks, three of them. One empty, more or less. The other two had taken on the by now all-too-familiar aspects of a pitched battle. To get to the Temple I'd have to cross the combat site.

I said, "They picked a good spot to kill each other."

"It almost would appear," the bubble mused, "that the Temple is under attack."

"Now that's just splendid," I said.

It wasn't the only thing on my mind. There were still too many unanswered questions. Blank spots in my brain. Why were there things I just couldn't remember? Like escaping the sloots in the jungle. Like digging for the bubble in the first place. Like Dr. Knox's role in all this. Somehow I had the feeling that Knox was in deeper than I recalled, only I couldn't put my finger on it. And what was so damn important about Lab Twenty-nine anyway? I'd find out. But first, Nina and Brent.

"We need a vehicle," the bubble said.

"Not thinking of taking off?" I inquired.

"On the contrary. We're going on in."

The car the bubble scanned was a two-seater warden patrol some blocks away. Only one seat was occupied when I approached, wrapped in my cloak. The lone warden conveniently slid down the patrol window to exchange words with a fellow law enforcer. "Yes?" he said eagerly. The stun gun gave him a quick, unplanned vacation. The ground was as good a place as any to dump him. I rode away in my prize.

"The radio," the bubble said.

I had little difficulty raising the Temple, which had nothing against an official visit. They were having enough trouble just holding the line, a voice explained through my receiver. Temple authorities would welcome some assistance in maintaining Temple sovereignty.

I gunned the patrol toward Temple-Wall-East; it slid up as my patrol scooted in, and down again. The war was behind me, the OW inner sanctum ahead. It was a sight I had always meant to take in, but not quite like this.

The hall pulsed like a heartbeat, a vast dome shimmering overhead. Colors seemed to melt through the air; sounds—vaguely musical—came with it. If you didn't look hard, there was no distinguishing right from left, up from down. The floor seemed to be a spinning pool of blackness under my feet. Interesting enough, in a mildly technical sense—only I had other things on my mind.

The two brothers-of-the-order who approached me wore long multi-colored robes that shimmered in the bouncy glare. They appeared to be striding through mid-air at first glance—an inspiring and thought-provoking spectacle—but it was merely a winding fiberglass ramp they walked on, and they ruined the effect at once by wringing their hands and going off on a long-winded complaint about property damage.

The sub-cults were behind the eight-ball when it came to property damage. No one in his right mind would think of harming an Anny brick: wardens would know what to do and be glad of the chance to do it. The larger sanctioned heresies, like the Incest Cult, had their own wardens too. But the smaller cults made do as best they could, relied on the good offices of the Annys and, when worse came to worst, submitted their grievances to an All-City Committee. For whatever good that did, which was never very much.

I cut short all the talk about property damage with a wave of my hand.

The bubble spoke:

"At the moment our primary concern is Schluss."

I added:

"Official business."

The bubble's voice was coming from my pocket pouch. Neither of the brothers batted an eye; stray voices here were strictly run-of-the-mill, it seemed.

"Schluss?" the shorter of the two asked.

"We request an immediate interview," my pocket pouch said.

"I see." The taller of the pair nodded and went away.

The short one commented, "an adept of the order, perhaps?"

"A dabbler," I said, and was rewarded with a knowing grin. I added, "The wardens outside seem to have the situation well in hand."

The brother had his doubts. "They tried to storm us," he said.

"The wardens?"

"The mob."

"Why?"

The brother shrugged. "Who can say? We did nothing."

"Perhaps that is why," the bubble said.

"You really are adept," the brother said.

The other brother came back.

"About this Schluss," he said. "There is no such Schluss here."

"You're certain?"

The brother was emphatic. "A Schluss was here. Seeking sanctuary. Our records show he remained with us two days. In contemplation. But then he left. He did not say where. Nor why. Suffice it to say he is gone." The brother spread his hands and looked appropriately blank. A stone wall, in fact, never looked much blanker.

The small brother lowered his head. "We do try to be of service," he murmured, "whenever possible. On behalf of our Temple, we express our regrets."

"Stun them," a tiny whisper projected itself in my right ear.

To hear was to obey. This bubble had the inside track—on some things, at least. I reached for my gun.

Darkness.

Someone had blanked the lights.

The two brothers were on me, or something was. I needed room. I flailed my arms. I got room. I used it to move away. I had no argument with this pair; I wanted to leave them before one developed. Any direction would do.

The dark held no terrors for me. I could take it or leave it. Any glink with a bubble could do as much.

A voice whispered in my ear. I followed directions. I was prepared to be led. I was grateful and eager for the privilege.

"To the left."

"You spoke to them," I said accusingly.

"Indeed I did. Most certainly."

"All right," I said, "I wasn't questioning it; I merely wanted to know why."

"Proof. For your sake, Norton. Bubbles have no vocal chords to exercise. It occurred to me you might approve. Objective verification. This should convince you of your sanity, at least."

"Actually, I was figuring my insanity had spread to new dimensions."

"Well, the two brothers were perhaps not the best subjects. Their life-style leaves something to be desired in the way of veracity. Still, they took my words at face value. Imagine, if you will, my dear Norton, a warden's reaction to a disembodied voice."

"I don't have to," I said. "The last one you chatted with wanted to shoot you. How much more of this stumbling around here?"

"There's a passage up ahead. Be content. They can't see you either. The two brothers, in fact, have gone off in another direction. At the Temple gates a mob is preparing to advance. I doubt if they can spare an extra brother at this time. You are about to bump into a door, Norton."

I put out a hand. In an instant I was back in a lit hallway.

"Take the stairs down. Two floors," the bubble said.

"What's there?"

"Your Schluss."

"Terrible, terrible," Schluss said, twisting his fingers. A tall thin man in his early forties, Schluss had thick lips, a longish nose, thinning black hair. His eyes, which were set too close together, were large and seemed frightened. "This unrest. How disturbing. How disquieting. It makes a shambles of one's nerves. It reaches into one's very soul, here even in the Temple, and brings the world's ills with it. What is the fighting like out there?"

I told him bad.

"I'd rather not know. Materialism. A poor foundation. Unworthy of man. Self-seeking, the inevitable result. What do you want?"

It was a small room. No windows. A cot. Nothing else. This wasn't going to take long. I only had a couple of questions.

"You spoke to Brent? To Nina Norton?"

Schluss seemed more frightened still. "The brothers let you down here?"

I said they had.

"What sort of sanctuary is this?" Schluss asked irritably.

"I'm the girl's brother," I said. "Brent and I work together."

"Your uniform—"

"Is just a cloak." I showed him. "I borrowed it to get here."

"You're not a warden then?"

"I'm a League historian."

"Your sister, you say?"

"That's what I say."

The tall man had reached a decision. "I'll tell you," he said. "Actually, we know each other, don't we?"

"I've seen you around."

"It's the cloak; it obscures you."

"It's supposed to."

"What can I say?" Schluss shrugged. "It's terrible. They took them both. Brent came to warn me. Yes, that's true. We'd worked together. He saw my name on the posted list. Saw it and found me here, where I often seek refuge. I was denounced, it seemed. That's common enough, isn't it? But where will I go now? He warned me. And then your sister came. That's all I know. They spoke together. Don't ask me why. I was agitated, distraught. Ordinarily, I am a man afflicted with a nervous temperament. My state of mind—you can imagine what it was. As I say, they conversed briefly. They left together. I saw them to the door. I watched from the Temple as they went down the walk. They were taken there. Perhaps they have already been released. I have no way of knowing. It was our own wardens who took them. Leaguers. Perhaps they were denounced too? Have you tried the stockade? That's the place to look, you know. If they're still alive, of course. Otherwise, there's always the cemetery, wouldn't you say?" He began to laugh. Tears ran down his cheeks. I left him that way, laughing and crying.

Back in the hallway, the bubble said, "You'd best shake a leg, my dear Norton. The mob has just demolished the front door. They will, I fear, not take kindly to your cloak. In fact, they appear quite infuriated."

"They probably have a reason," I pointed out.

In the twilight world between night and day, I tooled the patrol through avenues laden with the dead and dying. Main drives were clogged: overturned vehicles lay in mid-street; milling, frantic crowds formed senseless human barricades cutting the roadways.

Side-strips kept me away from the tumult.

The patrol attracted attention. Bricks, bottles, stones bounced off its smooth surface; bullets stung it, lasers seared it. I pressed down on the speed pedal and rode away from this outpouring of hate. They were wasting it on me. I shared their sentiments.

The stockade was a slab of metal, not unlike an upended match box, cheerless and windowless in the oncoming darkness.

The mob was there. As expected. The League stockade would draw the annys like flies to the sugar pile. Once an object of awe and reverence—the symbol of League justice—it now became a major target.

Floodlights glared in the east, lit up the square. The crowd huddled in semi-darkness near the west wall. Between it and the stockade entrance, two rows of glittering tanks angled north and south, formed a make-shift lane down which only authorized personnel might travel.

I rode the gauntlet unhindered, my patrol and black cloak serving as an impeccable pass.

A League warden waved me on.

I wasn't all that much of a stranger here. The workings of League justice had long intrigued me. All historians are given a thorough course in its administration, one that centers on this very building. The stockade was composed of courtrooms, cells, and execution chambers.

Parking, I took to a fast gait.

"Not that way, you fool," the bubble hissed as I turned toward a doorway. "That's the men's room."

"Sorry."

I found the right one and started up a staircase. Safer than the chutes.

The bubble observed, "Empty here. Once you step out, however, you will be inundated with wardens."

"That's not so wonderful," I said.

"I wasn't rejoicing at the prospect," the bubble said. "I merely informed you."

"Consider me informed."

The map in my mind told me some things, but not enough. I was on a side staircase in the east wing. The cells would be in the northwest sector, but they covered five floors. With all the gating the annys had been indulging in of late, the cells ought to be filled to bursting. How was I going to come up with Nina and Brent? How, in fact, was I going to go walking among all those wardens? The cloak had served its purpose; it had fooled them from afar. But I had neglected to change into the entire costume. A costly oversight, it seemed.

"What," I asked, "are the chances of your spotting Nina or Brent."

"Zero. I don't even know what they look like. The cells are a veritable hive."

"You've looked?"

"I gave it, as you would say, the once-over."

"Yes, I might say that. On a bad day. Your powers, I take it, don't extend to divining?"

"My powers," the bubble said, "are quite mundane."

"Too bad," I said with real feeling.

In the hallway, I was alone. I turned a corner and suddenly had a good deal of company. My cloak ended short of my ankles, and anyone bothering to look would see that I was wearing the wrong trousers. Wardens and execs were rushing in all directions, as though the stockade were a fish tank and someone had let in a shark. A face detached itself from this crowd. I recognized Gabler. The little clerk was striding straight for me. What in hell was he doing here? The system was certainly quakey when bureau personnel started turning up in the stockade. Things must be worse off on the walks than I'd realized. Gabler looked his usual fretting self and so far had neglected to notice me.

My hand reached for the first doorknob in view. A door came with the knob. I went in as Gabler went by. He hadn't seen me. At most he had glimpsed a cloaked back. I looked around to see where my feet had taken me. Suddenly I wasn't in that much of a rush anymore.

"Look at that," I said.

The bubble said, "Eh?"

I was in a wardrobe chamber, an oversized closet.

"Use your imagination," I said.

"It takes all my imagination just keeping up with you. Do try to bear in mind, my dear Norton, that I am unacquainted with the mores of your quaint environment."

"Coats. Cloaks. Robes. This is the first break I've had."

"My presence is the first break you've had. In any case, you already possess a cloak."

"A tribune's robe," I pointed out, "will get us into any cell on the premises."

"How could I possibly have know that?"

"It's longer too," I said, selecting a white one. "For the cell block, that's an improvement over this thing."

"Well," the bubble said, "if you can stop congratulating yourself for a while, you might try one on."

Back in the hall, I found I was walking a bit steadier. The tribune's robe evoked respect—or would, should the occasion arise. I appreciated that. Strutting around as though I owned the place, however, made me a standout. Everyone else I saw looked worried sick. I tried out a little gloom on my face and found that it fit. I didn't have that much to celebrate—not yet, and perhaps never. I was getting by on lift-o, nerve, and what still might turn out to be an overly chummy hallucination. By now I wasn't certain where one began and the other left off.

I knew my new attire was inspiring confidence when a smallish exec-type whispered at my side, "Can you hear the guns?"

The stockade was, among other things, soundproof. "No," I said.

"You can if you listen," the exec told me. "The guns are everywhere." That seemed true enough.

I found the processor's office. The wall clock said 7:48. The lights were on in the front office; the second room was dark. I went through a sheaf of yellow papers on a desk, inspected a ledger. I had stopped feeling regal again and my hands had started to sweat. I was hitting the ups and downs like a yo-yo. The weekly lock-ups were nestling in a green loose-leaf. The League might be lax in some matters, but they kept a tight rein on things that really counted: their lock-up roster was as complete and up-to-date as tomorrow's think-text. It took me twelve minutes to find Nina and Brent: Cell Block 7 and 7A. All I had to do now was get them out.

"Sorry, your anny," the warden said. "Those are orders. Cell blocks closed for the night. Why don't you come back tomorrow?"

If I came back tomorrow, I knew it would be as a resident. Glancing up and down the corridor, I saw that the seventh floor was a veritable wilderness on this side of the iron door. Just the warden and me. I made my voice confidential. "Let me show you something; you'll like it."

The warden looked interested.

"See this?" I said. I showed him the stun gun under my robe. He nodded. I pulled the trigger. He fell down. I forgot to ask if he'd liked it; he couldn't have answered anyway.

Dragging the warden into the cell block might have aroused the inmates; even the accused and guilty still harbored sparks of patriotism every now and then. I left him under a staircase after removing his key ring.

Opening the doors revealed a not-unexpected interior. Metal bars forming cages ran from floor to ceiling. Eyes gazed out at me from behind these bars. No talking; neither cheers nor jeers. Discipline was still too close to the Anny mold here. Time was needed to learn. What they ought to have been doing, of course, was screaming their heads off. They would probably get to it later.

The quiet was almost eerie. Eyes watched me, followed my movements. I could hear their breathing. I could hear my footsteps on the metal floor. Above me my reflection kept pace on the polished metal ceiling. The top of a lot of heads seemed to bob like hairy coconuts in an off-shore breeze. I moved quickly down the aisles. I didn't like this place. I'd be glad when I left it.

The first cells were segregated according to sex. After that, suspects—men, women, even children—had been pushed pell-mell into the same cages. Space at a premium. These cells were never meant to hold this many. A poor time for suspects. In our Annys, even on the best days, it could happen to anyone, like a virus—sudden and devastating—only a bit more permanent.

I found them where they were supposed to be, in adjoining cells. Efficiency. I'd called their names while still a cell block away, frantically following the markings on the walls. In the quiet it had been no more startling than a flock of wild broncos let loose. It brought out the murmur in the crowd—there's always one lurking just below the surface—and a restlessness began to crest like a wave. There's always that, too.

"What kept you, son?" Brent inquired casually, his unlit pipe between white teeth, his round, friendly face pressing the bars. He had thoughtfully made his way to the front of the cage on hearing his name called. Brent's cellmates looked me over in open consternation. They were a varied lot, a true cross-section of Leaguers. Whatever had closed in on them had been somewhat less than selective.

"I took the wrong ramp," I told him, working the key in the lock.

By the time his cage door swung open, I was down aisle at Nina's cell. She was farther back in the crowd, her gray-green eyes looking anything but cool now. They were large, moist, and seemed in shock. A reasonable reaction when you thought about it.

Black slacks, black blouse, hair turned gold against the silk of her costume—she emerged.

"It *is* you, isn't it?" she said.

It seemed likely, I told her.

Gazing into those eyes, I saw depths in the depths, not deeper than most, perhaps, but more interesting—to me, at least—and I knew why I'd risked it all tearing up the city to get here. Our embrace got more of a jostling than I'd expected. The rest of my sister's cellmates were pouring out, passing us on the run. Brent, at my side, summed it up. "Stampede," he said. The annys in his cage had already taken leave of their quarters, were racing down the aisle. A howl let loose from the other cells. I had hoped to keep things quiet. My intention had never been to spoil the aura of complacency that hung over this lock-up. I approved of it. For my purposes it was an ideal blanket under which I might snatch Nina and Brent to safety.

All that was past.

I tossed the key ring to a burly inmate as he rushed by. The inmate paused long enough to open more cells. The ball was rolling.

Nina said, "Jimmy, let's go!"

I was hesitant.

"Plans?" Brent murmured.

"Well?" I demanded, addressing the bubble.

"Why, in heaven's name, did you release the convicts?" the bubble asked from my pocket.

"Suspects," I said to the bubble. "Not convicts. What did you want me to do, leave them here? Anyway, they didn't ask my permission, if you noticed."

Nina and Brent stood staring in astonishment.

"You wouldn't believe me even if I told you," I said to them. "It's some sort of seeing-eye communicator and it's attached itself to me. Invaluable gadget. You ought to get one yourself, if there're any more on the market. You have any brothers or sisters?" I asked the bubble.

"I am an orphan," the bubble explained.

"He's unique," I said.

"Are you joshing?" Brent said.

"It talks, it looks, it listens," I said. "As far as I know, it doesn't walk. And it likes me. Don't you?"

"I shall be relieved when this relationship is terminated," the bubble said.

Nina grabbed my shoulder and shook it. "Stop it, Jimmy!"

"It has a will of its own," I explained, removing the bubble from my pocket pouch. "See? Say something." I held it between thumb and forefinger, letting the light catch it to good effect, revealing a perfectly empty interior, incidentally. It was as unlikely a bubble as one could hope to find.

"We're wasting time," it said.

"See?"

"I don't believe it," Nina said.

"I don't blame you," I said.

"What is it?" Brent asked.

"Damned if I know," I said.

I replaced it in my pocket.

"What does it want?" Brent asked.

"I don't know."

"It talks to you?" Nina said.

"It talks to anyone," I said. "You heard it."

"And you don't know why?" Brent said.

"That's the one thing it doesn't talk about."

"Why," Nina said, *"are we still standing here?"*

Around us the cells had emptied out, their barred doors open, a testament to the swiftness of change. Farther down the cell block voices still shouted. The metal ceiling reflected a dark, swarming mass over by the main door. The clang of distant cell doors served as a reminder of what I'd begun.

"We can't become part of the runaways," I said. "I didn't count on all these annys taking off. They'll be stopped. And even if they're not, it'll be a bloody mess. Clogging stairs, jamming chutes, bottling themselves up without any help from the wardens. What *we* have to do is find some other way out."

"Such as?" Brent raised an eyebrow. He was becoming excited. For Brent.

"So why aren't we looking?" Nina demanded.

"We're looking," I told her. "Take my word for it. That's what the bubble's for."

"That is not *quite* what I'm for," the bubble said. "Down below, your first contingent of suspects has poured out into the arms of the wardens. More wardens are on their way. We shall avoid that entire area."

"It really *sees* down there?" Nina said.

The bubble said, "There are twelve exit points in all. The farther away from the furor, the better. I have viewed each companionway. They all have their shortcomings. Exposure is a possibility at various junctures. One way, however, recommends itself. We shall take it, having little choice in the matter. Up the aisle, toward the rear. I'll tell you where to turn."

We started hiking. No annys were left to gape at us. We could certainly stand the solitude; as long as it continued, it meant the crisis was somewhere else.

A long way off a tiny bell began to tinkle.

The bubble said, "That makes it official."

The breakout was no longer news. Somehow I didn't feel reassured.

We were covering ground. The aisle had led to an outer corridor, then a staircase, the staircase to another floor, an empty one.

Lack of windows ruled out orientation. The bubble, however, didn't seem to mind. But why should it, I thought bitterly; what could happen to a bubble?

"We've reached a blank wall," Nina said.

"There is a passage in that wall," the bubble said. "It offers a guarantee of privacy. A slight depression a foot from the floor and an inch to the left of the corner. You will have to look closely."

Nina said, "Why is this taking so long?"

"The roundabout route is often the shortest," the bubble replied, "if I may be permitted to say so."

"I wasn't talking to you," Nina said.

I was down on my hands and knees fingering the wall; so far my luck had been less than spectacular. I said, "You might as well talk to him, honey; he's the only guide we've got. I can't find your damn depression."

"It is not mine, although it would be interesting to learn whose it is. A bit more to the right, my dear Norton. I see I have been promoted from 'it' to 'he.' I am most gratified."

"Here it is," Nina exclaimed, pressing a thumb to the wall.

"I don't see anything," I said.

The wall slid up into the ceiling.

"Thank you, my dear," the bubble said.

The wall slid back as we stepped inside.

"It's dark," Nina said; we moved ahead.

A faint glow issued from the walls, became brighter.

"Are we safe here?" Nina asked.

"As long as you remain in the city proper," the bubble said, "the word has no meaning."

We'd come out in an office, one decked in League gold. A desk no bigger than a small swimming pool. The windowless pattern of the building broken here by a view-screen focused on the outside world. Nighttime.

A gold desk-plaque read: DELL LANCASTER.

We looked at one another, and seven men stepped through a hole in the wall.

I actually heard the bubble gasp. It seemed to be an oversight on its part, all right. And the last one it would get to make through me.

None of the men was Lancaster. Two of the men held lasers. They came toward us, a big glink in the lead.

The view-screen became opaque. It did other things besides serve as a window. Lancaster's thin frame appeared on the screen. His deep-set eyes flicked over us, as though we were so much rubbish. Then he scowled.

"You," he said, sounding disappointed, somewhat puzzled.

I resisted the temptation to ask him who he'd been expecting.

"I should have known," he said bitterly.

"Known what?" I asked.

"You fact-lovers are all alike. Always wide on the think. You've broken into the wrong place, anny. This is a one-way walk—" The boss of all bosses was talking, and his errand boys were all darting quick reverent glances at his bigness. It was now or never.

Bringing my fist down on the big glink's gun arm, I smashed the laser out of his hand. Next to him, a beefy anny spun my way, bringing up his weapon. I hit him in the face. He fell down.

I moved now.

Banging two heads together, I drove a fist wrist deep into a stomach, popped a knee cap with one kick, caught an elbow with both hands and broke it.

A fist swung at me. Going in under it, I drove the edge of my hand at an exposed Adam's apple, saw the fist become an open flabby hand, its owner twirling away.

Two pairs of arms grabbed me; I brought a knee up into a groin, dug out an eye with a finger, and the arms all let go. I swung a left at an unshaven face, a right at another. The faces vanished. A short glink rushed me and went over my shoulder.

A shoe in the ribs took the wind out of a burly type, who bounced away like a rubber ball.

As I moved sideways, a laser burned my cheek. That was cheating. I broke a chair over a head, and the laser stopped doing it. I picked up a short body and tossed it at a skinny one. They went down together.

Someone was screaming, the party with a smashed arm. I rammed his head into the wall to quiet him.

I broke a leg that was kicking at me, sliced at a stray neck as it whisked by, took a knife away from a hand by twisting it. Bones grated one against another.

Teeth, I noticed, were biting into my arm. My fingers tore away part of a lip and the teeth let go. The face looked funny now. Blood spilled down its chin. I smashed the bulbous nose flat and it looked better.

Driving my heel into a cursing mouth on the floor, I saw teeth scatter on the carpet. A metal cigarette stand in my hands took away part of a head. I swung it again. An arm snapped like a match-stick. I left the stand wound around a pair of quivering shoulders. I sank a fist into a splintering cheek, hacked away with open hands at a chest, rib cage and spine, heard sounds like gears meshing together. And over that, the last of the screams and groans.

A body dragged itself across the blood-stained carpet toward a laser. I stomped on it and it stopped. A short, bulky glink came off the floor to make a run at the weapon. I hammered his jaw as he went by. He crashed into the desk.

I was laughing now. The sound spun around the room and climbed up the walls. I looked around for more excitement. I liked what I was doing. I wanted to do more of it. There was no one left to play with, nothing standing, anyway. I kicked at an arm, put a foot into a face. Nothing moved. Nothing stirred. I had run out of bodies just when I was getting the hang of it. They were scattered over floor and desk, stretched out in various poses and postures of recline, like so many paste-up figures.

I looked up at the viewer. I wasn't quite alone. I had forgotten Lancaster. He was still there, staring out of the view-screen. His mouth hung open. His eyes goggled. Slightly bent forward at the waist, he was peering out at me—unmoving—as if he were encased in a block of ice.

It was a rather shocking exhibition at that.

The viewer went black.

I looked around. Nina and Brent were gone. Talk about shocks.

The bubble's voice came. "I've sent them on ahead. Hurry."

A hole still in the wall. I hurried. "It was a trap," I told the bubble. "Why didn't you warn us?"

"I didn't know!" the bubble wailed. "Somehow they blocked me . . . somehow . . ."

As I ran through the dark passage toward the garage, another thought struck me.

What I had just done to those glinks had been simple, smooth, and pleasurable. I'd managed it—effortlessly—with my bare hands. A nice piece of work—for a gladiator!

But *me?*

For me it was *impossible!*

Fear hit me like an exploding wave.

Something began to peel back in my mind.

"It would be best not to remember." Dr. Knox wiped the perspiration from his haggard, bearded face. The eyes, behind the glasses, were round, terrified. His short squat body shook. "Wouldn't you say?" he added, seeking my approval. I didn't like the idea, but what could I do? Still, I wasn't certain that blocking a segment of my mind was the answer. The Cope-Con was in an uproar. Knox and I had taken refuge in an office. At best we had only minutes. The lights were out. Knox kept lighting matches. Erlich stumbled through the door, his face yellow in the flickering match-light. He gaped at us. Knox told him to get out. Something that sounded like a cannon had begun to boom. This time they really meant business. This time they were out to kill us all. I felt the net growing tighter. Mind blocked, I'd be moving half-blind; the handicap might prove too much. But I had to act. "All right," I told Knox, "we'll do it that way." The match flickered out. When light came again, Knox held a match in one hand, a watch in the other. The watch hung from a golden chain, swung back and forth. I watched it swing . . .

The passage had come to an abrupt end. I touched a wall.

"They've turned off all power," the bubble voice came out of the black. "The panel will not open automatically."

That was great. "What do I do?"

"Use your laser, Norton."

I'd even forgotten I had one. But then I'd been forgetting a whole lot lately. I brought the laser into play. The bubble said, "Put a shoulder to the panel now!" I did, and was back in a lightless garage.

The bubble talked me to a vehicle and directed me as I aimed it up a ramp. I held my breath, but it was only a formality. The bubble might have slipped up on the trap back there, but aside from that it was batting a thousand. For a piece of glass, it was doing a man's job.

We sailed out into the night. I could see why no one had gotten in our way.

Fire.

The mob danced around the burning stockade, now a giant sacrifice, beating at it with flailing limbs, a thousand mouths twisting in a scream that was a chant of triumph; the flames licked at the mob, and it swayed back and then forward again. The night, the howling crush, and the flames had acquired a unity, a life of their own.

I rode away.

Bonfires made up of manors every ten, twenty blocks glowed a cheerful red, turned the walks into a lunatic's version of playland.

Looting everywhere.

Small groups worked patiently in metal screens that guarded mart fronts. Friendly wardens could be seen lending a hand. The barriers had come down; anny mixed with anny, all colors and armbands.

A lone siren still blared from the northwestern part of the city, as if crazed by the violence it was witnessing. The lights had failed on half the walks. Some showed no signs of damage, lay calm, untroubled, in a midnight slumber. Others were wrecks. Water splashed along pavement from broken hydrants.

I didn't have to ask where Nina and Brent had gone. I knew. I just asked if they'd gotten there in one piece.

"They have," the bubble assured me.

Good. I had an errand to make before our second reunion.

I found him in his bedroom, the beard pointing straight up at the ceiling as though the mischief had come from there and he was helping to expose it. The glasses at his side were cracked, his eyes open. Slippered feet aimed toward the window. But whoever had done this hadn't used the window. The front door had been open.

The Leaguers had gotten their man.

No trial.

No stockade.

The moment had called for harsher justice.

Dr. Knox had paid the price for his heresy.

And the rest of them were probably netted too. All the top men. Perhaps even Holden Weber himself.

I stood very still. I could kill with my bare hands, but I had no memory of acquiring such a skill. I had asked that my mind be shielded against itself and I couldn't even remember why.

Knox knew, had held the key.

Now the key was shattered.

FLEISHER SIX

THE SHAKEDOWN

Boris Goren had an office in the East Forties. A secretary ushered Eddy Fleisher into his presence. A small, bespectacled, narrow-shouldered, grayish man of anywhere between forty-five and sixty, Goren half rose, extending a small limp hand across his desk.

Fleisher took the hand and pumped it enthusiastically.

Goren, nodding him to the chair facing his desk, made a steeple of his hands and said, "From Mr. Kraft, is it?"

Fleischer said it was.

"A fine man, Mr. Kraft. I do not believe I have ever had the pleasure . . . the privilege . . . of a visit from one of Mr. Kraft's representatives."

His voice was high tenor, but low on inflection. It came out flat, as though Goren wasn't quite interested in what he was saying.

"The truth is," Fleisher said, "I'm here on my own hook."

Goren's round face, with the small graying Hitler mustache, showed polite interest. "Well, that is undoubtedly somewhat of a change. I would almost suspect, Mr. Fleisher, that it is an error . . . yes, an error . . . While I am a board member of United, it is my practice to leave the . . . shall we say, day-to-day operations . . . indeed, the security details—for that must surely be uppermost in your mind, coming as you do from the Agency—to those whose direct responsibility it is. Yet I am always happy . . . indeed, delighted to make the acquaintance . . . to meet, under any and all circumstances—"

Fleisher interrupted him: "I don't think so."

Mr. Goren's mouth, under the clipped mustache, parted; he closed it. "What?"

"No," Eddy Fleisher said, shaking his head, "you'll hate it."

"Hate what?" Boris Goren was obviously at sea. His visitor helped him out:

"You'll hate meeting me. You'll wish you never had."

Goren laughed. In the silence that followed, Fleisher said, "One of U. T.'s employees, an Earl Kneely, has been helping himself to company property, Mr. Goren. He found his way into your safe, in that office you keep down at the tool works."

"My safe?"

"We've recovered a substantial portion of the goods, however."

"The goods?"

"Haven't been around to the old plant lately, huh?"

"Why, no . . . You say you've apprehended the culprit, Mr. Fleisher, and recovered the valuables . . ."

"Not exactly. Kneely's still loose."

"Well, now—"

"But we can lay hands on him whenever we want."

"Then I don't see—"

"Hold it. We've got some of the stuff back, but not all of it. We think we know where the rest of it is. But that's not what I'm here about."

Boris Goren shrugged. "I am truly at a loss . . . you have me at a disadvantage, Mr. Fleisher."

Eddy Fleisher agreed with him:

"You bet your sweet ass I do."

Goren blinked at his visitor, removed his spectacles, looked at Fleisher, returned spectacles to nose, and fidgeted.

Fleisher, taking out a white alligator-skin notebook from his coat pocket, waved it at Goren. "You see this?"

Goren saw it.

"Know where this comes from?"

Goren said nothing.

"Your safe, that's where. And before that? On Joe Smiley, the *late* Joe Smiley I'd guess. So I'll tell you how it is, Goren. You can play it one of two ways. It's up to you. Either I take this and its mate to the DA, or you cough up twenty-five grand."

Goren flushed. "This is unheard of—"

"You're hearing it now," Fleisher said. "This once and no more. So let's can the chatter. Like I said, Goren, it's either yes or no." He slipped the book back into his pocket. "I may be barking up the wrong tree. That's okay too. This stuff may mean nothing to you. Then you won't care what I do with it. But if this means something, then beating around the bush won't help. It won't get you anywhere. Your best bet is to talk turkey."

"This is an outrage," Goren said.

"Then I'll go."

Goren almost yelled it out:

"No!"

Fleisher grinned at him. "Now you're getting the hang of it," he said pleasantly.

"It is utterly preposterous to assume that I would have the slightest interest—"

"But you're willing to come across with something?"

"What you suggest is out of the question; I might conceivably . . . for the sake of mere argument, Mr. Fleisher . . . make you an offer . . ."

"You're wasting your breath. Twenty-five grand will make it right; not a cent less."

"You are insane!"

"Sure. Only look at it from my angle. I've either got you over a barrel or I haven't. Now I'm betting that if the DA starts digging into this, he's going to come up with plenty, so it'll cost you even more, won't it? Listen, I'm taking a chance bracing you like this; it could mean my license, maybe even the pen—if I'm wrong. So I'm not in this for nickels and dimes. You can see that, can't you? I'd be a sap if I settled for anything less. I'm not going to do that."

Goren said, "Ten thousand is all that I have . . . all I can raise."

Fleisher laughed at him.

"You'll beat the chair, all right. Unless the DA comes up with Smiley's body and digs your slugs out of him. But somehow, looking at you, Mr. Goren, I'd imagine that's kind of unlikely. You're not the type to turn your own trick, are you? But I figure once they start nosing around, they'll get enough on you to send you over for a good long stretch—"

"For God's sake, ten thousand is my limit, I swear to you—"

"Yeah, they'll throw the book at you, Mr. Goren, and all because of a measly fifteen grand. It's a hell of a time to go scotch with the roll, Mr. Goren. But that's your look-out—"

"Twelve thousand, Fleisher; that's every last penny I've got."

Fleisher grinned good-naturedly:

"Uh-uh. That's what they all say. It won't wash, Mr. Goren; I've checked."

Goren's voice came out a strained whisper. "You must give me time . . . I need—"

"A good mouthpiece if you don't come through. Sure. I'll give you till tomorrow at twelve, let's say."

Goren half rose from his chair, his face a pasty white. But Eddy Fleisher had already used up all his arguments. He raised a hand.

"Save it," he said. "Another word and you'll have me cryin' in my beer."

Putting a hat on his head, he left.

Eddy Fleisher lit a Camel and rode down the elevator. Humming a snatch of "Lovely To Look At," he walked out the front door and into the rain. He didn't open his umbrella. Instead he went quickly around the block and into its back alley. Trash cans lined it; timber for some construction project lay in it in a moist heap. Neither cat, dog, nor person had seen fit to invade the alley's privacy. Rain made it Fleisher's private domain now. The door was there. He went down a flight of stairs, smelling oil, gas, turpentine, paint. The boiler room, ringed by flimsy wooden partitions, led to a half-empty coal bin; a lightbulb shone dimly overhead, making the coals look like black diamonds. A water faucet trickled into a rust-stained sink. Fleisher went into a larger room. Three tiny windows high up on the right wall let in a miser's portion of daylight. Two metal sinks were at one end of the cellar. Pipes ran along the ceiling. Something leaked up there. This scratching through the depression, Fleisher reflected, wasn't worth it. A row of fuse boxes stood out high on the east wall, at right angles to the sinks—small gray monuments to the utilities, one of the few going concerns.

Sig Woolsey, using an orange crate for a seat, nodded. A slender, sharp-featured man of twenty-eight in a peaked cap and worn leather jacket. Woolsey took the earphones off his head and turned to Fleisher.

Fleisher ground his cigarette stub against one of the round columns that appeared to hold up the ceiling, put a shoulder against it and sank both hands into his coat pockets.

He said, "Goren start dialing?"

"Three, four minutes ago," Woolsey replied.

"One call?"

"Uh-huh."

"Say anything?"

"He's going somewhere. No names. Some broad. No destination."

"That's okay."

"He sounded plenty skittish."

"Did he now?"

Woolsey, digging out a flask from a hip pocket, unscrewed the cap, took a swig, capped and returned the flask to its resting place. "Yeah. Got enough?"

"Some names would've helped."

"I'd guess," Woolsey said. "Who you got on it?"

"The professor's in a doorway across the street. And Sweeny and Jud."

"Going to join the chase?"

"You kidding? One squint and Goren makes me. It's back to the office; this field work tires a man. Pack it in here."

"That's okay with me."

Sig Woolsey got busy.

"We got him running," Fleisher said hopefully.

Back at Kraft's, Eddy Fleisher, draping coat and jacket over a hanger, opened his umbrella to dry, loosened his tie, rolled up his sleeves, put his feet up on the desk. After a while the phone jingled.

"Eddy?"

"Yeah?"

"Sam," a voice said.

"How's the man, Sammy?"

"Eddy, I been trying to get you."

"I was out. What's cooking?"

"You should only know."

"A pot full, huh?"

"More even; you I'm not steering wrong."

"That's nice, Sammy. So?"

"You maybe remember DeKeepa?"

"It's a cinch I won't forget him."

"You can forget him."

"Yeah?"

"It's hunky-dory now."

Eddy Fleisher looked at the phone as if it had grown teeth. "Don't tell me—"

"So if I shouldn't tell you, why am I wasting a nickel? He's dead, Eddy. Somebody an ice pick put in his back."

Eddy Fleisher said nothing.

"Hello, Eddy—"

Fleisher said:

"When?"

"This morning, they found him."

"Where?"

"On Park Avenue, near 54th Street."

"Anything else?"

"No, Eddy. You should pardon me. Between you and DeKeepa was bad blood—"

"DeKeepa was a louse."

"This is general knowledge. So why in your voice there is no smile?"

"It's in hock, Sammy."

"Times are so bad?"

"Even worse."

"The policemen—you are maybe worried about them?"

"The hell with them. If I had a dime for every guy in this business who'd tangled with DeKeepa, I could retire right now. Forget it."

"Tsk-tsk, Eddy. You keep such loose company for a fine young man. But as long as your conscience is spotless, eh?"

"It's in cold storage. Thanks, Sammy."

"Take care, Eddy."

"Yeah."

He hung up.

The phone rang again around five.

"This is the professor," the professor said. "I have completed our little chore."

"Where are you?"

"In the Bronx." He gave an address. "Our friend Goren is visiting someone on the second floor. He was observed entering Apartment 2A, which can be viewed from the street door, and was."

"Who lives there?"

"A woman, according to the mailbox and bell. A Miss Nancy Ward."

"Is Lou Sweeny there?"

"Sweeny, Jud, and I."

"Okay. You and Jud stick around. If Goren comes out, let Sweeny take him. You got that?"

"Right-o."

"Anything else?"

"He gave us a merry sleigh-ride, he did."

"Spot you?"

"Doubtful."

"Just playing it safe?"

"Let us say he took no chances."

"Okay, I'll see you in a jiffy, Prof."

"We'll be waiting," the professor said.

NORTON SEVEN

THE LAB

Rea said, "Nothing." Her black hair still tied in a bun, her narrow face tired.

Max Gordon agreed. "Not a trace." He peered out through the brownstone's window, his wide belly pressed against the sill, the white T-shirt stained and wrinkled, his large walrus mustache immaculately groomed. A shotgun lay on the living-room table.

I looked over his shoulder.

Nothing was the word.

On this block three street lamps still burned, the rest having been mangled in the shoot-out. Three were enough to show the burned-out buildings, the pock-marked pavements, as if a sudden disease had wasted the district. But the other structures were still, miraculously, intact. Lights burned behind flowered curtains. An occasional anny patroled the street. Unpacified. The block still belonged to its dwellers. The wardens had unloosed their destruction and moved on. If their intention had been to return and finish the job, it had been thwarted. The wave of violence that had gutted the city had undone all such plans.

"They won't be back," I said. "Not for a while."

"We'll be ready," Max said. "You can count on that."

I went back up the stairs. In the room, Nina asked, "Jimmy, how did you know we were in the stockade . . . your bubble?"

"It helped," I said, "but you folks left a trail."

"The whole thing was an error," Brent said. "I admit it. I should have stayed home."

The story was a simple one:

Brent, spotting Schluss on the posted list, had set out to warn him, a humanitarian act. But Schluss—always the fatalist—in true Other-Worldly fashion, had declined to run. Brent's own name had also appeared on an advance listing, perhaps because of his connection with me, perhaps on his own account. Nina, checking the proofs, had come across it and left her office determined to find Brent before the wardens did. They'd run out of luck together.

I said, "Any trouble getting here?"

Nina said none.

"The bubble thing told you, of course," Brent said.

I shook my head. "I guessed. Where else would you go?" I said to Brent. "Right?" I asked the bubble. There was no reply. "It's sulking," I said.

"What is it, James?" Brent said.

"Mass hypnosis, probably. Ask it. It talks a great line."

"If you boys weren't all shell-shocked," Nina said, "you'd be worried."

"I'm worried," I said.

"One thing," Brent said to me. "Where did you pick up all that muscle-power? Or did I dream it? We left in the middle."

"You didn't dream it. I don't know."

"I've never seen you do *that*," Nina said.

"Neither have I," I said.

"The bubble helped?" she said.

"It's not talking."

"It was talking all right a while ago," Brent said. "It was going the whirl."

"That was a while ago," I said.

"Did you insult it?" Brent asked.

"Did you hurt its feelings?" Nina asked.

"I don't even know if it has any feelings," I said.

"Perhaps you ought to apologize?" Nina said.

"All I did was ask it some questions," I said.

"That's all?" Brent said.

"We had a slight disagreement."

"With your brain trust?" Brent said.

"I don't really think of it as my brain trust. Strange as that may seem."

"Maybe you should?" Nina said.

"Look," I said. "For all I know, maybe it *is* my brain trust. And yours. And everyone's. Who knows? I don't, that's for certain. For some reason, back at that Cope-Con, I had Dr. Knox fooling around with my mind. *I asked* him to, you understand. Only I can't remember why. 'It' knows, I guess, but it's not saying. Also, for some reason, which again the bubble doesn't see fit to elaborate on, I'm now to take off for Lab Twenty-nine."

Brent said, "*Where?*"

"A Cope hideaway. If it hasn't been exposed by now. But I'm not going. That was the essence of our dialogue. If the bubble stays mum, I go my own way. That makes sense, doesn't it?"

The pair both said that it did. They said it almost in unison.

I sighed. "It seems to me that you folks aren't taking this with the proper measure of seriousness."

I told them some of my other troubles: the beating I'd given to the boys in the stockade wasn't my first winning bout. I'd been jumped by sloots after escaping the Cope-Con and—I now believed —I must have freed myself from them the same way. *Only I couldn't remember.* The bubble fooling, somehow, with my mind? Why? And why wouldn't it tell me? I shrugged. There were too many whys for my taste.

"Your plan?" Brent said abruptly.

"The mountains. I've got the passes. Safe Conduct. Bought them months ago, for the three of us. Foresight, huh? They'll see us through."

"H-m-m-m," Brent commented.

The bubble said nothing.

Brent went away to his own room.

I went to the closet and undressed, hanging my clothes on a peg. When I turned back to the bed, I was nude, but Nina wasn't. She lay there, her gray-green eyes wide, fixed on me, her long blond hair stark against her black costume, lips parted in a half-smile. "I'm not going to," she said. I understood. The last time we had neglected the ritual. We wouldn't now.

She tried to kick, but I grabbed her foot, my hand pinning her shoulder to the pillow. "I don't want to," she cried. Sliding my hand up under her blouse, I found her breast. "No," she moaned. "No, don't!" I took her blouse away from her. She was perspiring slightly now, her cheeks flushed. Slowly, I moved my hand down her belly. She tried to squirm away, but I was holding hcr wrists in one hand. I forced her back against the pillow. She wriggled against me. My hand went over her smooth stomach, moved on slowly below her navel. "Oh!" she cried. I took her slacks away. She had nothing on underneath. A series of faint ridges showed on her waist where the elastic had pinched. She was breathing through her mouth now. She lay spread out under me. I held her with a forearm against her throat, while another arm pried her legs apart. She twisted her hips under me, trying to get away, but I wouldn't let her. She began to scream now and that was good, for that was part of the ritual too.

Rape.

Rape.

Rape.

We played it often.

Were good at it.

Excelled at it.

But then, what brother and sister weren't?

It was morning when we awoke.

Brent, I found, was gone. The bubble was gone. So were our safe-conduct passes. And that made it a clean sweep.

It was one surprise more than I needed—or could stand. This was really the finishing touch. The low blow from left field. And what made it worse was its total lack of rhyme or reason. There was only one thing left to do now. And I aimed to do it. Get out. Get out fast. In a way I was almost glad: now it would be all over.

The short glink stepped out of a doorway as Nina and I were leaving Gordon's house.

"I got business if you want," he said.

"What kind of business is left?" I asked.

"Credits are still worth something," he said. "Credits are the whirl."

"Of course," I said, "but what would they buy us?"

"Whaddya in the market for, friend?"

"Shooting the loop."

"Gating it, eh? Where to?"

"Say the mountains."

He shrugged. "Let's say that. Sure. If you got the credits, friend."

"I've got them," I said.

"Fifty of 'em?"

I nodded.

"Well," he said, all smiles. "That's the whirl. What are we waitin' for?"

"You taking us?"

"Not me, friend. I'm just the middle glink. It's a business, see? A lotta annys gonna be stuck now, gonna need a hand, right? So some of the boys are cupping the sweets: credits for service, see? It's a good shake, friend; a steal at the price. And I ain't blinkin' you either . . ."

The small glink in the too-long garments and crooked nose led the way. He moved slowly, as a blind man might, but his head kept twisting from side to side, his eyes darting. Nina and I trailed along behind him, my hand on the laser in my jacket pocket. A tank would have been better, but the laser was all I had.

Other annys moved on the walk, not many and in groups. Their eyes told of the *change* as they raked each passerby, bored into every doorway and alley. It was every glink—every clique—on his own.

In the raw daylight the city looked like a scraped bone.

"This way," the little man called.

We left the walk, followed him into a courtyard, through a doorway. We went down into a basement. The brick walls were damp, cracked. Another door took us outside again through a narrow alley between two brick walls. A final door and we were in another building, another room.

Dr. Corpious turned from a table.

"Ah!" he said, wagging his three chins at us in obvious delight. "I do so approve of happy endings." He beamed at us.

"Remember Dr. Corpious?" I said to Nina. They exchanged hellos. "You wouldn't think it to look at him," I continued, "but he cuts a dashing figure on a race course."

Corpious rolled his eyes heavenward, wagged his beard. His voice was a low rumble. "I bow in disgrace. That you should have witnessed so unseemly a rout. One of my very few, I assure you. But who would believe Corpious? Bah!"

"The others wing it?" I asked.

"They looped Verrik."

I tut-tutted.

Corpious spread his hands. "The perils of our trade."

"What happened?"

Disgust showed on the good doctor's face. "An electro-eye, no less. To be *exposed* by an amateur contrivance! Unmanly. What brings you here, Norton?"

I looked around. Our guide was gone. I said, "The little glink promised us safe conduct."

Corpious beamed. "Yes, indeed. I have scattered my faithful cadre throughout what—uh—remains of the city. To offer assistance in whatever meager ways are still possible. How delightful that I can be of service to *you*. You are bound where?"

"The mountains."

"Ah! That would be sixty credits. And well worth it."

"It used to be fifty."

Corpious looked sad. "Inflation. We're upping the go."

"I thought he robbed only the rich?" Nina said.

"Mere public relations, my dear lady," Corpious said.

"What about it, Corpious? Can you take us on?"

"Assuredly. Money is king. The mountains it shall be."

"You're staying put?"

"I remain. It's a time of flux; there are droppings to retrieve."

"Good luck," I said, "it's all yours."

"About Brent," he said. "You go your separate ways?"

I asked him what he meant.

"He came to me this morning," Corpious said, unrolling a map. "Look. Here was his destination. The mountains, too. But what an unpopulated, barren spot."

I looked at the good doctor's finger, saw where it rested.

"Lab Twenty-nine," I said to Nina.

Nord sat hunched over the wheel, silently peering ahead through the windshield. The roadblocks had disappeared. Coalition brown loomed before us. Not too much the worse for wear. All the sectors hadn't suffered equally. Most structures here looked whole. Wardens still manned watchtowers. I wondered if the new utopia might rise from those towers? I hoped not.

We passed the Federation next. It was in tatters. No one in sight. We said good-by to it, rode by a charred, green Alliance. No one asked to see our pass, no one bothered with inspection. Soon this was behind us too. We left the city. No-man's-land was a pile of rubble. Not so long ago, I'd come crawling over these ruins. Things had looked bleak then. I didn't know if they were any brighter now.

Nord said, "This stretch is loopy."

We were on the wild strip, hunting grounds of every maniac in the area. Ransomers. Slavers. Revengers. Sloots. I said, "Can we go it?"

"Not if they got a cannon."

"How would they get a cannon?"

"Then we can go the slam. It's a flip. Car's armored."

"We're safe," I told Nina. "Give or take a bit."

We reached the forest. Trees on either side of us. A wide strip of broken concrete before and behind us. No other vehicles on the road. Nord opened her up. We bounced along. The ride hadn't been comfortable to begin with—it was worse now. The car careened past ditches and dugout, one-time home of booby-traps that added zest to a spin in the country. The strip wore the scars of dozens of pitched battles. Nature and time had done the rest. It was no place to stage a race, but crawling along would have been just as risky.

We were bound for Lab Twenty-nine.

Nina said, "Brent has always been close to my heart, Jimmy."

"A good man," I agreed.

"He must have known what he was doing."

"No doubt."

"He probably had good reason."

"Let's hope so."

As we rode, glinks took pot-shots at us, threw sticks, stones, and even themselves at our car. It was expected. We ran over them. No cannons materialized.

I turned to Nord. "You going back on this obstacle course?"

"That wouldn't sweat me none," he said. "Not with old beauty here." He patted the wheel reassuringly. "I keep driving. Corpious got a stash up in them hills."

"Gets around," I said.

"Sure. He got a business to look after."

We began to climb short rises, then higher ones. Attacks from the environment began to diminish. The terrain was actually starting to look pretty. We went up a small mountain. Below us a multi-colored forest stretched out on all sides.

"Getting a look at the world?" I said to Nina.

"I could do without it," she replied.

Lab Twenty-nine was on a hill. No one but our Copes used the gravel road that led up to it. A steep, almost vertical decline ended in a tree-swept valley to our left. A wall of trees on our right.

We pulled up in the driveway.

The lab was stone and mortar. No sign of any life. The Copes, a going concern yesterday, were only good for memoirs now. The lab was an anachronism, relic of a dream that had gated.

"Want me to wait?" Nord asked.

Nina said, "If no one's here, Jimmy, do we have to stay?"

"We don't have to anything. But this is as good a spot as any. Better than most, probably."

"I'll wait," Nord said.

"Of course," I said. "It can't hurt."

"Won't the League find out about this sooner or later, Jimmy?"

"I doubt it. Why should they bother? They've got better worries."

Nord grinned. "You figure the Annys for folded?"

"Most of them."

"There're other cities," Nord said.

"There's Europe," I said. "Asia. Africa. Whole continents. You know what's going on over there?"

"How could I?" Nord asked.

"Neither do I."

After the first blight, communications had broken down totally. Those first years had seen Annys spring up everywhere. But now? No one knew, and it didn't matter either.

Out of the car, Nina said, "What do we do, just walk right up?"

"Think Brent's going to blast us?"

"I guess not."

"He's probably not even here," I said.

We started toward the lab.

"Jimmy, can we trust him?"

"Who—Nord? I don't see why not. He's been rather good. Took a chance coming out here. Besides, we don't have anything worth stealing."

I looked back. Nord was seated in the car, staring impassively through the windshield.

I took Nina by the arm. "Just think of this as a picnic."

"I've never been on a picnic."

"Make one up."

A peculiar whistling sound rose up over the trees. Grabbing Nina, I fell to the ground. Behind us something went smack. I looked back. The car was gone, a hole in it's place. I heard a voice coming from nowhere. "Whatever you do," the voice told me, "remain perfectly still."

I remained perfectly still.

Someone was laying down a barrage around the lab. But the bull's-eye on the car was all they had to show so far. Lab defenses had sprung up; shells were bursting against an unseen but sturdy energy screen. A little late for Nord, but perhaps the rest of us still had a chance.

The voice said, "All right now. Move."

We moved.

We ran for the lab and into it as doors sealed shut behind us.

"Join us," the voice said.

"It's your friend the bubble," Nina said.

I'd already gathered as much. Brent met us in the control room.

"Ah," he said. "The pilgrims arrive."

"Two-timer!" Nina said.

"Now, now," Brent said. "There must be some reasonable explanation for what I've done."

"There would be," Nina said disgustedly.

The control room was dome-shaped. Sunlight shone through it. Walls were lined with machinery, dials and knobs. They hummed.

I said, "What's the shooting?"

"Leaguers," Brent said.

"It's fantastic," Nina said. "All the way out here."

"Not so fantastic," I said. I was suddenly very tired. I sat down on a chair. "How long have we got?" I asked the bubble.

"Perhaps fifteen minutes."

"Can we hold them that long?" I said.

"The defenses are automatic. They should suffice," the bubble said. "But Lancaster himself is heading the charge."

"*Lancaster?*" Nina said.

The bubble said, "He may have resources we are unaware of."

"What, for God's sake, is going on here?" Nina demanded.

"Our James," Brent told her, "is a more important glink than meets the eye."

"He's right," I heard myself say, "now that I think of it."

"Well, go on, tell me," Nina said.

"All right," I said, "meet Holden Weber—the man in the black mask."

Nina looked at me. "Weber? He's supposed to have founded the Copes."

"Take it from me," I said, "he founded them."

"And you're Weber?" she said.

"I'm Weber. It's just a name, honey."

"But how could you—"

I knew what she meant. Weber had had a reputation as a great scientist.

"The bubble handled the science end of it," I explained.

"The bubble?" Nina asked.

"Yes," I said, feeling even more tired. "Meet Norton Fifty-nine, alias the bubble."

"Well, none of it was my idea," I said.

"I don't get it," Nina sighed.

"I don't blame you," I said. "I almost don't get it myself. How are we doing out there?" I asked the bubble.

"They are unable to penetrate our screen, as yet."

"That's nice. How much longer?"

"Ten minutes."

"Ten minutes *what?*" Nina asked. "And what's the bubble doing with our name, Jimmy?"

"It's his name too," I said. "He's our descendant. We're his ancestors."

"You're telling me he comes from the future?"

"No," I said, "he doesn't come from there; he *is* there. And some future it is."

"Pure hell," the bubble agreed.

"All we get," I said, "is the voice. Along with a few scientific tidbits."

"I thought you didn't know who this bubble was," Nina demanded.

"I didn't. That is, I knew and then I didn't. Nothing to it, really. As Weber I built the Copes, the bubble doing the real work through me; it had contacted me years ago. Well—somehow, the opposition got a *fix* on the Weber part of my mind. Just prior to the raid on the Cope-Con. The bubble clued me in. They could trace the Holden Weber mind configuration. They had a way of doing that, it seems."

"That's impossible," Nina said flatly.

"I know. But they did it. A tracer of some sort. It could pick me out in a crowd. Not that they knew *who* I was; the game would have been long done if they'd known that. They had this finder wide open when they raided the Cope-Con. Knox blanked my mind of the Weber part. As long as I didn't remember Weber, I was safe. Knox never knew I *was* Weber. I just told him to knock out all information pertaining to Weber in my mind. He did, figuring I knew too much and wanted a safeguard in case of capture. He was right, too."

"I don't believe it," Nina said.

Brent said, "If you can believe in a talking bubble, my sweet, you can believe in anything."

"Where is it?" I asked.

Brent removed the bubble from a coat pocket, tossed it to me. "Just something to center a voice on," I said. "It's a piece of glass. Any object would do. In the past a cigarette lighter served the cause. But the girl's got a point."

"Thanks," the girl said.

"Norton Fifty-nine didn't do anything radical to my mind," I said.

"I merely instructed him how to release some of his potential," the bubble said. "Under stress man can do wonders with what he has, lift impossible weights, perform incredible feats. Years ago, when I first communicated with Norton here, I instructed him in self-hypnosis. Gave him a subconscious key that would trigger his mind, release his powers."

"That's how I beat the sloots," I said, "and worked over Lancaster's men. The bubble was able to keep my mind blanked during the former tangle, but in the stockade some memories slipped back; I was dangerously close to remembering the whole thing. If I could remember how I got my powers, I'd remember I was Weber too. And the opposition could trace Weber."

The bubble spoke: "It is a riddle. A nasty one, to be sure. Trace Weber? Indeed, it *does* smack of the incredible. They have also discovered a way to partially block my vision. It was all I could do when the sloots chased him to summon Norton on the unconscious level."

I said to my descendant, "Incidentally, where were you when I needed you most? You were gone for a whole stretch back there."

"I was under personal attack. We have five minutes."

"Norton Fifty-nine's world is a bit untidy," I said.

"A hell-hole," the bubble said.

"Let's not go into that now," I said.

"Why did Brent take the bubble?" Nina wanted to know.

"It told me to," Brent explained.

"And our passes?"

"Those too."

"An error," I told her. "When Knox buried the Weber part, recall was tied to this lab. It was all one package. Again, Knox didn't *know* what the lab was, just that it existed, and I wasn't supposed to know that. It was a slip, but we were in a hurry back there; the Leaguers were knocking at our door. So we hustled. In fact, too much was screened from my mind. That's why I walked into the Justice Hall at the Pen estate. Forgot the damn spotters in there. Rush jobs are no good. Anyway, Norton Fifty-nine couldn't tell me the lab's function—or much else—without restoring my Weber-memories. In the city, or anywhere else, that would have been the end. We were only half a step ahead of Lancaster as it was. So the bubble had Brent take our passes."

"How did he know we'd follow?" Nina asked. A logical mind.

Brent said, "I arranged it with Dr. Corpious. He was *my* friend too, after all. You don't think we'd leave that to chance, do you? One of the doctor's boys were waiting for you."

"But we didn't have to take up his offer," Nina said.

"But you did," Brent said. "The bubble and I agreed that you two would follow me, James."

"Why?" Nina said.

"Because," I said, "they had me figured out."

"So what *is* the lab's function?" Nina said.

"Time travel," I told her.

The lab began to shake.

"What are they doing now?" I said.

"Something different," the bubble replied.

"They seem to be getting results."

"More noise than motion."

"Well," Nina said, "I must be missing a point somehow."

"No," I said, "I left that for last. The idea is—I fix up the mess."

"Mess?"

I waved a hand. "The bubble's. Ours. Everyone's."

"He doesn't want much," Nina said.

"My dear," Norton Fifty-nine told her, "Where I am, I may be the only rational creature left. Certainly one of the very few. I am a scientist living in what to you would be the far future. To me it is—regrettably—the unpleasant present. I am surrounded by an age of unspeakable barbarism. Mere terror and violence in the world which I inhabit would be a blessing. We have yet to achieve it, so low have we sunk.

"I was part of a small scientific community. Scientist is a word, however, that only vaguely describes my preoccupations. We had at our disposal a vast store of knowledge, gleaned through the ages. But we were quite unable to stem the tide of onrushing darkness. Disaster struck more than once, until finally, after a lengthy and depressing period, I was the only capable researcher left among our tiny community. Our adversaries are by no means incompetent. And while much in my age is merely bestial—and repulsively so—there are vile enclaves over which our adversaries rule that are, at least technically, quite proficient. It is they who challenge us.

"There may, of course, be other centers of civilization still in existence—here, somewhere—but I have been unable to contact them. At this moment I am relatively secure in our fortress, which is surrounded by an energy field more advanced but not unlike the screen that shields you.

"For generations this fortress has labored single-mindedly to produce the apparatus through which I now speak, and the concomitant matter-transmitter. On its success and the success of your mission, my dear Norton, hangs the fate of nothing less than civilization itself. I trust I have made myself clear . . . ?"

"Civilization," Brent said. "Well, as long as it's nothing petty."

The glass dome overhead was beginning to cloud over. The sun was blinking out.

The bubble sighed. "We have reached the intermediary stage. We are secure from Lancaster's assault. My time is short now."

Nina looked up at the opaque dome. "Now what?" she said. It was another logical question.

"The matter that's being transmitted is us," I told her. "And the lab is the transmitter. In fact, it's the reason behind the Copes—only they never knew it. Just carrying out the bubble's orders, I'm afraid. We're going back, through time, to the place the bubble thinks all this started."

"He's not certain?" Brent asked.

"Even my viewer has its limitations," the bubble said. "There is interference. I can only speculate."

"Look," Nina said, "why doesn't the bubble go back itself, for goodness sake? I mean why send *us*?"

"I should never, at my age, survive such a trip," the bubble said. "And if I did, who would look after my charges here? I can hardly abandon them now. In any case, this operation demands a young, pliable type."

"And Jimmy was the *best* candidate?" Nina said in some wonder.

"I was almost the *only* candidate," I told her.

"Initial contact could only be made with a direct ancestor," the bubble said. "Gene congruity, you see—the DNA factor—is necessary for vocal transmission."

"So if it weren't for the Incest Cult, the direct link," Brent put in, "you'd *never* have reached James here. Or anyone."

"Precisely. Of the ancestors I was able to view with some clarity, Norton here was the most promising."

"Sure. I was always promising something or other."

"The Copes, at first, appeared to be merely another fledgling cult," the bubble said. "Then they became a formidable heresy, one spread far and wide, concealed by the best that science could provide—that, in short, *I* could provide, through my ancestor here—without alerting the powers that be to my intervention—"

"A smoke screen," I said, "to build *this*. The Copes provided the manpower, the materials; as Holden Weber, I directed things. No one knew the real purpose but me. That way, we were almost safe."

"So what *is* this purpose?" Nina demanded.

"You are going to eliminate a proto-ancestor," the bubble said. "Dig up the roots and the tree withers. Destroy an ancestor and the entire line dies. It will change the course of history."

"Won't that change you, too?" Brent asked, "and us?"

"At the moment, I am not part of history. Or time itself. The energy field that surrounds me is a total entity. When your task is realized, I hope to return to what, I trust, will be a more suitable world. In your new environment you people will be extrahistorical, not subject to the chain of history. I think. Take no unnecessary chances, however."

"He *thinks*. Do we return here?" Nina asked.

"Alas, the time apparatus is one-way."

"I won't mind that," Nina said. "Whom do we kill?"

"That," the bubble replied, its voice fading, "is what I'm not sure of. Does the name 'Grace Waller' mean anything to you?"

"A minor ancestor," Nina said, "of Dell Lancaster."

"Find her," the bubble said, "and kill her. You might also look into something called United Tool . . . Good-by . . ."

"Good-by?" Nina said.

The bubble didn't answer.

I went and got the bag of money that I'd prepared long ago. We were ready.

The lab was there.

Then nothing except a sort of milk-white opacity that offered no diversions for mind or eye. That went too.

We were standing on a grassy field, waist-high in weeds, looking up at the stars. There were a lot of them, and frankly we were glad to see them.

Brent said, "Say something to the bubble."

"Why don't you?" I asked.

"I'm afraid it might not answer."

I called the bubble's name, which was easy since it was my name, only with a number after it.

Nothing happened.

"I'm cold," Nina said.

I gave her my black warden's cloak. She wrapped it around her and we had the small satisfaction of solving our first problem in our new world.

Brent sighed. "Well?"

I nodded gloomily. "Maybe he'll get through to us later."

"You honestly think so, Jimmy?" Nina asked.

"Honestly? No. We're probably on our own."

We had popped up in a place called the Bronx, as we later learned, and in a way we were fortunate. Materializing in Times Square would no doubt have led to a lot of complicated questions, and at that moment we were conspicuously short of answers.

We hiked around until we stumbled over a highway. By that time it was starting to dawn. We hitched a ride, only it was going the wrong way—away from Manhattan. This Manhattan was a great word, and both Brent and I grew to enjoy using it. There had been no Manhattan where we'd come from, but at least we knew about it. Nina was at a slight disadvantage. However, for all three of us to have been professional historians would have been stretching a point. Anyway, she caught on pretty fast. The girl had a head.

"You with the circus, brother?" the driver, a friendly chap who smoked a briar pipe, inquired politely.

Well, we weren't dressed properly for these parts, that was certainly clear.

"Actors," Brent told him.

"Ah!" the man said, as if that explained it.

We were let off at one of the streetcar lines in a quiet residential section.

"That was pretty easy," Nina said.

"I'm afraid it's only the beginning," I pointed out.

FLEISHER SEVEN

THE SQUEEZE

Manor Avenue between Watson and Bruckner Boulevard was a quiet, tree-lined street.

Eddy Fleisher, having pulled up, sat waiting in his car.

The professor, in a long tweed overcoat and narrow-brimmed sportsman's hat, came over, climbed into the front seat.

"Goren took off about half an hour ago," the professor said. "Sweeny stuck with him. No one has entered or left the building since then."

"Where's Jud? He packing a rod?"

"On the corner. I think not."

"You?"

"Negative."

Fleisher reached into the glove compartment, removed a gun. "Give this to Jud. There's probably going to be a wrangle."

"Yes?" The professor seemed mildly interested.

"Odds have it that Goren's run to the top with his little problem since I made it into a whopper. So the top it is. What's out back of the house?"

"There is a fire escape." The professor had an objection: "You will be in plain sight of anyone happening to glance out the back window. Across the yard, there are trees out there that act as a buffer, but not sufficiently to do you much good."

"That doesn't matter. Two to one they'll figure I have every right to be there. Wouldn't you?"

"No."

"You've been corrupted by the trade, professor."

The professor put Fleisher's gun into his coat pocket. "I see," he said.

"You go back to Jud, lend him the hardware. I'm taking the fire escape up. Give me three minutes. Then Jud uses the downstairs buzzer. If no answer, he puts a bullet through the lock and comes up anyway."

The professor slid out onto the street. "You are a callow and headstrong youth," he told Fleisher, "and I hope you know what you're doing."

"So do I."

Only one room was visible from the fire escape, a dark one. Fleisher raised the window, looked over his shoulder. A row of windows across the way looked back. He put a foot over the sill. Inside he made out a bed, a closet, a dresser, a closed door. Somewhere in the flat's interior, a buzzer sounded. Jud downstairs. Fleisher inched open the door. A rectangular line of light outlined a second door at the end of a corridor. When he heard knuckles rapping on wood— Jud in the hallway—Eddy Fleisher slid his gun off his hip and stepped into the lighted room.

Jud's lanky figure stood framed in the hall doorway.

Two men caught Fleisher's eye:

One, short, stocky, in rumpled white shirt and baggy pants, had opened the hall door. His hands were empty. The other, tall, in dark suit and hat, was behind the door. He had a gun.

The short man was saying, "Sure, come on in." His voice sounded friendly.

Jud came in. One hand stuck in his yellow raincoat pocket, his eyes darting to left and right.

Eddy Fleisher said, "Lift 'em."

And the lights clicked off.

Eddy Fleisher went sideways and down, rolling as far as he could away from where he was.

Gunfire! Loud, insistent.

Someone was screaming.

Eddy Fleisher lay still, hoping that if he lay still enough the people who were shooting would stop.

They stopped.

Racket enough to account for a squad of marksmen, but that obviously wasn't the case. Someone, Fleisher knew, whom he had missed had doused the lights. The room wasn't big enough to hide a platoon. Best to make himself small. Logic and reason said so, and this was no time to challenge the higher faculties. He hugged the floor, trying to hear what he might. The screaming was done. Jud, along with everyone else, was playing Indian. He hoped.

Time crept by like a crippled spider.

Slowly, the hall door began to creak open. No hand or body was apparent. With the opening came light.

Four dim figures were now visible.

One, Jud, was flat against the floor, to the far right of the door.

Short and squat was over by a wall.

The man in suit and hat was sitting on the floor. He had his gun, aimed at no one in particular.

A woman crouched near a light switch, behind Fleisher.

A voice from the hall called:

"Police!"

A gun thudded to the carpeted floor. Others followed it.

The professor came through the door. "You certainly make a lot of noise," he complained.

Eddy Fleisher, on his feet, said "Hello."

"I would have looked foolish shooting them with my finger," the professor said.

Jud had his gun out.

The man in hat and suit slowly righted himself.

It was Tom Lacy.

"You son-of-a-bitch," Eddy Fleisher said.

"Honest, Eddy, it didn't mean nothin'."

"You were gonna burn me down, you stinking ragbag."

"Jeez, Eddy, you know me; I wouldn't—"

"You'd ax your own mother, you rotten grubber. Who's this?" indicating the woman.

"Aw, that floosie—"

"You shut up, you!" the woman shrieked.

A washed-out blonde in her late forties. Eddy Fleisher had never seen her before. Short and squat was a stranger too.

"It's her dump," Lacy said.

Fleisher said, "You're Nancy Ward?"

"I ain't got nothin' to do with nothin'," the woman said emphatically.

"You were merely waiting for a street car, my dear," the professor said.

The short man said, "If you guys are cops, I want a mouthpiece."

"We're the rubout squad, punk," Jud explained.

"Don't give me that crap," the short one said. "You're cops. I can smell cops."

Fleisher said to Lacy, "You got one chance: you shoot your yap off good, loud and very clear."

"Who are you gents?" the woman asked.

"Pigeons," Jud said.

Tom Lacy raised his voice: "You think I don't know you had me tailed? I ain't that dumb! You never did nothin' for me. You was playin' me for a sap, Eddy. Me, that never done you no harm. Ain't that right? It's the truth, ain't it? You was gonna take back the boodle, too."

"Maybe. But you're singing the wrong tune," Fleisher told him.

"We had better shake a leg, Eddy," the professor said. "You folks made too much noise."

"If you ain't cops, who are you?" the short one asked.

The woman said, "I was doin' a favor for these gents, that's all."

"You going to spill it, Lacy?" Fleisher said. "It's that or the kiss-off. You name it."

The professor said, "Shoot him or make him sing. We haven't all day, Eddy."

"You heard the man," Fleisher said.

"I'm packin' it in," Lacy said. "It's all yours, Eddy. Only I ain't got that much, honest. You ain't gonna believe this; I know you ain't. It's screwy. But last night, after we sprung Earl, I got home, you know; it was almost mornin'. And I tried to get some shut-eye, see? Only this dame shows up outta nowhere; she comes bargin' in. I ain't never laid eyes on the twist. But she knows all about me; what's what and who I pal with; you know, the works. This frail, she's tellin' me all about myself, right? She shoves me to the window; I gotta take a look-see, she says, so I'll know she's levelin' with me, that she's on the up-and-up. I look an' I make this ghee; he's over there in the doorway across from where I jungle up. From Kraft, the skirt says, the ghee's from Kraft. Just like you, Eddy, she says—Eddy Fleisher's from Kraft, too. She's got the inside track on all our scores, about Earl beatin' the tool works, about his gettin' collared and us helpin' him amscray, and how we divvy up the take three ways. She says I ain't gonna keep none o' that loot unless I put the chill on you. That's what she says. And she shells out five grand to prove it; it's a set-up, see? A soft trick. She gives me the where and when—here, now."

Eddy Fleisher said, "You saw her when?"

"Nine-thirty, maybe ten in the mornin'."

"You did, huh?"

"Honest, Eddy."

"Come off it, Lacy; that's a line of crap. Even I didn't know I was going to be here then."

"Cross my heart, Eddy. Ask Denney here; he'll tell you."

Denney, the short, squat party, agreed. "I got the pitch from Lacy, say, around eleven."

Eleven had Fleisher at the corner chop house. "Still too early," he said.

The man called Denney shrugged. "What's that to me?"

Eddy Fleisher asked, "What did Lacy say?"

"Say? What's to say? There's this chump needs puttin' out and could I use some action. Sure, I say, only it'll cost a G. That's too stiff, he says. All I gotta do is kibitz. The sucker can peg him, so I gotta make with the door. That's all. We settle on five C's. Two-fifty down and the rest when the bum's stretched."

Fleisher said, "That's me, the bum."

"So what?" Denney said.

"I'd never've crossed you, Eddy," Lacy started to whine, "if you'd been straight with me."

Fleisher turned to Nancy Ward. "What's your spiel?"

"Half a yard. You don't get rich on that mister, do you? That's for this dump. And for being blind, dumb, and deaf. That's what you want?"

"He called you?"

"Yeah."

"When?"

"Eleven-thirty."

Fleisher said to the professor, "This has to be the bunk; it's too goofy. But why cook up a yarn in the first place? You don't have to con a stiff; this bird was all set to drill me."

"Aw, Eddy—"

"Better keep it buttoned," Fleisher said.

A siren began to wail somewhere a long way off.

"The Johns," Denney said evenly.

Jud asked, "We turn 'em in?"

"Gimme a break, Eddy," Lacy said.

Fleisher said, "Willing to kick back your end of the take?"

Lacy said, "Anything. Anything at all. You call it, Eddy; I'm your boy—"

"Clam up, chiseler. You go with him, Jud; see he delivers."

Jud said, "I say turn 'em in."

"The sirens, Eddy," the professor said.

"Where does that get us?" Fleisher asked Jud. "Yeah," he told the professor, "we'd better hustle."

"Through the window?"

"Right-o." To Lacy he said, "This jane that engineered all this, she got a name?"

"Sure; you bet."

"Well—you going to make me ask?"

"Hell no, Eddy; Grace Waller, that's her tag. Honest to God, that's what she gave me: Grace Waller."

NORTON EIGHT

TRANSFER TO YESTERDAY

We caught the trolley, after a twenty-minute wait—a rickety, creaky affair—transferred to another, had our transfers punched, and boarded still a third before we got where we were going.

"You with the circus?" a woman asked us.

We remained actors and clowns until a little after nine o'clock that morning, when the stores opened. Both Brent and I bought ourselves thirty-five-dollar gabardine suits. Nina showed up in a wide-shouldered string knit dress, a felt hat with a parasol brim. Two cents got us a newspaper. A tourist map of the city told us where we might find the apartments to let that we came up with in the paper. We settled for a couple in a rooming house in the East Thirties. Nina and I rented it as man and wife. Brent went down the hall.

"One thing," he told us. "No more of this rape ritual. That's out. Incest is taboo here."

"Taboo?" Nina said. She seemed shocked.

"Absolutely!"

"How vulgar."

"Well, that's the way it is. You've got to keep it quiet here. You're married—"

"Of course we are," Nina said.

"But you're not brother and sister."

"In my heart," Nina said, "we'll always be brother and sister; it's better between brother and sister—"

"Keep it in your heart," Brent said.

During the next two weeks we did everything but move into the 42nd Street Public Library. It became our home away from home, our instant university, our passport to the new world. We had a lot of catching up to do. We caught. Each morning the three of us polished off breakfast at a Third Avenue cafe and hiked up, under the rumbling el, to the reading room. We splurged on newspapers, magazines, brought home a radio, and even went to a movie, something with a Mae West. If we were going to do any good at all, we'd have to know our way around, at least in a rudimentary fashion.

It took a while.

Opinions in our day were traps. Heresy lay beneath the surface of any argument. Listening devices stood ready to record and classify every syllable.

Mid-1935 was a madhouse of rhetoric, a deluge of raised voices and pounding fists.

Worry was our response at first. But we got used to it.

In our day we'd known our Anny and its immediate neighbors; knowledge had ended there. Now, for the first time, we could listen to a foreign language being spoken. It broke us up. The Leaguers had clowns who mimicked other Annys; but this was *it*, down to the cockeyed gibberish, the wild gesticulations.

The old signposts had vanished.

Starting from scratch, we worked our way through a pile of books like kids cramming for the big exam. The books—mostly—told the truth. It was a change.

Through all this we ate as much as we could, sampling everything, without becoming candidates for a stomach pump. Food had been at a premium back when; it alone was worth the trip.

Brent turned up with two women during the second week.

In the third week our rooming house blew up.

We were late in arriving home that night; it had saved us. The horse, an old nag, had hauled its ice wagon onto the trolley tracks. The hand of the bubble? We never knew. The ice man finally coaxed dobbin away. We continued our bumpy ride and got back to our rooming house barely in time to see it disintegrate, the blast shaking the block. We stood on the corner of Third Avenue and Thirty-third Street and looked at the damage, the flames and smoke.

"Let's get out of here, James," Brent said. That was wisdom. A crowd was gathering. We moved into it and away.

"Got your bank books?" I asked.

They did. We'd banked our fortune. The rest of our possessions were replaceable, but manufacturing more cash would have been a hardship.

"Someone knows about us, Jimmy," Nina insisted.

Difficult to refute.

"How could they?" Brent asked.

"What do you think?" I asked.

"I don't," Brent said.

I didn't either.

"Perhaps a gas pipe blew up?" Brent said.

"Perhaps the Annys are just a bad dream," I suggested.

"Maybe this is," Nina said.

I said, "You know, we have an ancestor here too, somewhere—a proto-Norton. I'm afraid we'd better have someone look him up."

"Really?" Brent said. "That's a bit far-fetched, isn't it?"

"Just playing it safe," I said.

"We're all far-fetched," Nina said.

"Have a seat, Mr. . . . er . . . Norton."

He waved me to a comfortable-looking black leather armchair in front of his desk. I took it.

"Now then . . ." he said, tilting his head a fraction to the right. He tried a smile on for size; it looked as reassuring as a cobra nodding a friendly hello to a potential dinner.

"I've got some work for you," I told him.

George DeKeepa bobbed his head politely.

"A good deal of work," I added.

I was rewarded with a genial grin. "Just what is the nature of this . . . er . . . work, Mr. Norton?"

DeKeepa was a large, fleshy man of forty-five or so, in a brown suit and a yellow and purple tie. The hands he clasped on his shiny desktop were thick, the nails carefully polished and manicured. His complexion was ruddy. A black pencil mustache made a straight line over full lips; thinning black hair was combed back, glistening under the overhead lamp-light. The collar of his white shirt cut a faint pink line around the thick, muscular neck.

We were on the fifteenth floor of the Flatiron Building. Two red-curtained windows looked out over Manhattan's East Side. Three-twenty in the afternoon, no sun shone into the wide, amply-carpeted office, but the day outside was bright and shiny.

I told him what I had in mind:

"I want United Tool watched."

"United Tool? The Corporation?"

"That's right."

"Watched, you say . . . er, Mr. Norton."

"That's what I said."

"All of it?" he laughed, "or just part of it?"

"The entire works."

"Well," he said jovially, "you're at the wrong place, that's for sure. You want the U. S. Army, not a gumshoe."

"Make that the top bracket. The governing board, the president of the company, his staff. It wouldn't hurt to do some looking at the administrative offices, either. And the plant itself out in Brooklyn."

DeKeepa screwed up his eyes. "You forgot the rest of the country. United Tool is all over the place."

"We'll begin here, and spread out later if we need to."

"Yeah," George DeKeepa grunted. "We looking for anything special?"

"General information. A rundown on the top brass. Whom they know, where they go, their sources of income. Less thorough on the subordinates. And a going-over of plant operations, too. That should do it."

"Strictly routine, huh?"

"For now," I said.

DeKeepa slapped his knee, put his head back and roared. "That's a good one. Strictly routine. All right, Mr. Norton, what's this really about, or did you come here just to shoot the breeze. I'm a busy man, Mr. Norton."

"I meant just what I said, Mr. DeKeepa, and I'm willing to pay for it."

"Is that so?"

I nodded.

"A dossier on all of 'em, huh? Do you for one moment, Mr. Norton, realize how much that would cost you?"

"I believe I have an idea."

"Heh-heh," he simpered. "And you've got that much money to throw around, have you?"

I reached into my jacket pocket, removed the wallet, got the check out and gave it to him. It was certified.

DeKeepa made a whistling sound with his lips.

"Twenty-five grand," he said.

"Enough?" I asked.

"Yeah," he said, "I guess you do mean it."

"I mean it."

"Yeah . . . but why? What's it all about?"

"Let's say I'm interested in starting my own company," I smiled. "I want to see how it works."

DeKeepa fingered the check. "No. Let's not say that, Mr. Norton."

I shrugged. "Say what you want."

"Look. I can't run all this down myself—"

"You've got an agency here—"

"Sure, but—"

"Pull them off what they're doing and put them on this. Farm out some of the work. I don't have to tell you your business. There's more money where this came from."

His voice was tight. "Where'd it come from?"

I just grinned at him.

"Come on," he said, "you can't expect me to go into this blind."

"Put it down to curiosity. Perhaps that's what I do for enjoyment."

"That's one maybe too much, Mr. Norton."

"Why?"

"Because all this you want will take more than a little digging. It doesn't have the makings of a neat job. And we'd be going up against the big money. They're bound to tumble."

"So what?"

"Trouble."

Street noises found their way up from the pavements below, came into the office through the window. I noticed a pigeon perching on the window sill. Where I'd come from there were few pigeons: they'd all been eaten. I said, "That's what you're being paid for."

"To take a beating?"

"To do some looking, that's all."

"Sure," he said bitterly. "All I gotta do is take on United Tool."

"Too much?"

"Damn right."

"Very well," I said. "Forget it." I put out a hand for the check.

"Don't rush so, Mr. Norton. I didn't say I was turning you down."

"It sounded that way."

"I didn't say that. It's just that all this is a lot to swallow in one gulp."

I said, "If I'd wanted to advertise my reasons, I'd have gone to a newspaper."

"Very funny, Mr. Norton," DeKeepa said, looking glum. "You're not making my job any easier. Only I'd be a chump to turn down this kinda dough. I'll have to hire some outside help, and it could run to an even bigger bundle"—he tapped the check with a thick finger—"before we're through. It's a helluva thing tangling with that bunch."

"But you'll do it?"

"Sure, I'll do it. But I won't like it, I can tell you that."

FLEISHER EIGHT

BENNY MOON

The rain had stopped.

The streets shone wetly, gaily, under the glow of yellow street lamps. A wind came off the East River, sent odd ends of refuse scurrying over the pavements. Foghorns moaned away the long hours of the night somewhere out on the river. Mist tumbled through the darkness, lit by street lamps, headlights, the silent scream of blinking neon lights. Streetcars clattered along in a spray of electric sparks, the wires overhead sinking back into the blackness. Newsies hawked tomorrow's press: *The News, Mirror, Herald Trib, The Morning Journal. The Times* was late. Pale window shades and frilly curtains clad the drab fronts of tenement houses, spilled weak light onto the fire escapes. Horse-drawn wagons creaked by with their loads of junk, fruits, vegetables. High above, the els roared their reports of progress and movement over the city's rooftops.

Eddy Fleisher did the poolrooms.

Faces peered out at him through waves of cigarette, cigar smoke. Wood clinked against wood, rolled over smooth tables. Voices reached him—murmuring, whispering, bragging voices.

"How's it goin', Eddy?" a pale-faced youngster in shirt sleeves asked.

Eddy Fleisher said okay. "Benny Moon around?"

"Not tonight. Try Piggy's."

He tried Piggy's.

The proprietor himself gave Fleisher the word: "Uh-uh. Maybe later."

Eddy Fleisher walked up a flight of stairs to get to Studs' Parlor.

"Oh, yeah," Studs said. "I seen him, all right. Stick around, maybe he'll be back."

Fleisher, touching two fingers to his hat, said, "Gotta eat."

"If I see him, I'll let him know."

"Fine. I'll be at Lipsky's later."

He went back down, out onto the street, ate without incident at a dingy chophouse, went out again.

Lucky Lipsky's was a basement dive. Fleisher, taking a corner table, nursed along some Johnnie Walker.

Benny Moon stepped out of the men's room. "As I live and breathe," he said, feigning surprise.

"What's your poison?" Fleisher asked when Moon pulled up a chair.

"Some of the white."

A waiter brought it over. "Cheers," Moon said.

Benny Moon, a lean, nervous man of thirty-five or so, always had a toothpick bobbing up and down between his narrow lips.

Fleisher said, "I want to see Felix."

"Berger?"

"Yeah."

"He's holed up."

"Yeah."

"Someone maybe's tryin' to put the slug on him."

"Well?"

"Can do," Moon said.

"That's what I figured."

"Fleisher's okay, Felix said."

"Uh-huh."

"You wanna see him now?"

"That's the idea."

"Follow me," Benny Moon said.

NORTON NINE

THE HIDEAWAY

Our second new home was on the fourth floor of a walk-up, one block north of Houston Street.

I joined Brent at the window. An aged junk peddler in a scraggly gray beard was leaning on his pushcart below. Kids in knickers played at stick ball.

Five-thirty in the afternoon.

After a perfunctory rap on our door, Felix Berger entered with a large, muscular man in tow, one Ralph Moody.

Moody, a Berger sleuth, quickly began to relate an incident: he had been digging into the Grace Waller affair when Berger shifted him to Glenway Norton, a bank clerk absent from work—without explanation—for over two days. At Norton's rooming house Moody had learned nothing he did not already know. From Norton's neighbors and fellow employees the detective had obtained a list of friends. This list also proved worthless.

The following day Moody began checking on the errant bank clerk's movements for the past week and made a discovery: others had also been showing interest in Glenway Norton. A neighborhood grocery clerk, the postman, a newspaper dealer all recalled, among others, a woman who had been doing some looking more than a month ago; her description—to Moody's amazement—rang a bell.

Grace Waller!

A photograph of the woman verified Moody's guess. It was the closest Moody had come to her in three weeks of steady hunting. As for Glenway Norton, he remained unaccounted for.

Berger lit a cigar. "Who is this Glenway Norton—a cousin or something?" Berger asked.

I put a yes to that.

"The *accident* in your other flat," Berger said, "you think it was an accident?"

"No."

"That's what I figure," Berger said. "You folks are getting too close. Maybe your cousin's in it too, huh?"

It was a thought.

A black-curtained touring car we'd rented whisked us out of town. The Manhattan skyline was gone in the night; in its place, open countryside. A few sparse houses set back from the roadway—these too were soon gone. Occasional filling stations, small restaurants gave way to long stretches of empty roadside. Underneath us concrete turned to tar, tar to gravel, and gravel finally to a bumpy, winding dirt path set between what seemed to be miles of trees, two walls on either side of us blotting out sky and stars. The odor of outdoors drifted in through a half-opened window. We had been riding for over an hour. Headlights picked out tree trunks, leaves, shrubbery, made them glitter like green gems against black velvet. The trees had sheltered most of the dirt path from the slanting rain that had fallen earlier. We came to its end. Brent killed the engine.

"Let's go," I said.

Piling out of the car, we went; Nina and I had hand guns, Brent a rifle. Long-nosed flashlights put two small circles of brightness at our feet.

All manner of sounds now. Most strangers. The night belonged to crawling, creeping, slithering things. We were trespassers here, intruders. I hoped we weren't the only ones. We reached a clearing. Waist-high foliage sprayed moisture over us. The air was damp, heavy with odors.

We heard the shot then.

It came from up ahead and slightly to the right.

Dousing our lights, we used hands and feet to guide us. We made as little noise as possible. There was no profit in rousing the enemy.

A little of this and we all but stumbled into a man-made clearing. In the moonlight we saw a log cabin, some fifty yards diagonally across. A grassy lawn, with no intervening shelter, made an oval around the cabin.

Anyone wanting to cross the clearing would do so in the open.

Something moved on the far side of the cabin.

Brent shifted his rifle. Putting a hand on his arm, I motioned with a nod of my head. Brent, Nina, and I stepped back into the forest.

I whispered: "Let's not rush it. If we work our way around, perhaps we can spot them."

Some forty-five minutes—and a couple of dozen scratches—later, our expedition had uncovered five men, all watching the cabin, all armed.

None had noticed us.

They were strategically posted around the cabin, covering its sides; each was alone.

There were possibilities in that. We decided to explore them.

The first person we approached was spread flat on his belly, rifle in hand. We came up behind him.

A sound stopped us. It was a familiar, reassuring sound:

Snoring.

I hit him in back of the ear with a gun barrel.

We had neglected to bring rope. Torn strips of our victim's jacket did just as well.

Our second effort found an upright target.

"That you, Jerry?" the target asked, not bothering to look.

It wasn't and we proved it.

Number three got off a yell and a shot before we clipped him. Shots and noise, it seemed, were a commonplace in these woods. No one came to his aid as Brent and I beat him unconscious.

That left two.

We found them together.

I lost a second knocking my two companions groundward.

I rolled clear as gunfire put holes into the earth around me; my gun, roaring back, hit nothing. Nina fired once.

A man pitched against a tree, sank to his knees, lay still. The other had taken a step into the moonlit clearing. An error.

Gunfire leaked twice from the cabin. The man in the clearing fell down.

"Hold your fire!" I yelled. "We're friends."

A voice from the cabin told us what we could do with that. It was a long and profane message.

Rounding up our three remaining captives, we presently marched them out ahead of us, their hands bound behind them.

"Don't shoot," I yelled, training our lights on our prisoners; the sight they made, I hoped, would be startling enough to give a moment's pause. It was.

"You know them?" I yelled.

He knew them and said as much.

"I'm going to take a chance now," I yelled. "Don't do anything rash; we're on your side."

Brent held the light on me while I dragged the two bodies out into the clearing. They were just so much meat.

I yelled. "You got one, right? We got the other. That should prove something."

His voice called back. "How do I know yours is dead?"

I emptied my gun into the pair; then, tossing it away groundward, I raised both hands high over my head and, spotlighted by two flashlights, began walking toward the cabin.

Glenway Norton said, "Who are you?"

I told him, "Norton's the name."

Our car was back on the highway, Brent lounging in the back seat, rifle on lap, proto-Norton between Nina and me. The night was a long, black streak outside the car windows. My foot pressed down on the accelerator. Our cargo of thugs was still back in the woods; we had left them there after finding their car and disabling it. I had asked questions and gotten answers. The answers meant nothing. The trio had been hired by one of the dead men to murder proto-Norton. The dead man was a local East Side hood called Frank (Gimpy) Souly; no one knew who had hired Souly. That didn't matter much. With Grace Waller in the picture, the conclusions were obvious. There was nothing in lugging our trio to the law; it would have been more trouble than it was worth. Our only chance was steering clear of all authority. We left the hoods to fend for themselves.

Glenway Norton said, "At least the name's familiar."

He was a tall, broad-shouldered lad of twenty-five or so with unruly blond hair and an open, boyish face. Sometime during the last ten days he had become aware that persons were seeking him. Fitch, the corner newsie, had been approached, and so had Kubicheck at the grocery store. Proto-Norton discovered he was being followed. Someone else might have run to the police, but not Glenway Norton. The situation intrigued him, and he made a game of it. He had, as far as he knew, nothing to hide, nothing to fear. That had been his mistake. On a whim he had led his pursuers a merry chase, wanting to see how far they would go.

They had gone all the way.

Hunters and quarry had ended up at Glenway Norton's country retreat, a tract of land he had purchased only last summer and on which he had built a cabin.

He said, "There are deer up in those woods, and I had planned on a summer of hunting. I'd stored a couple of rifles in the cabin, lots of shells; the place was stocked with canned food; I even had three jugs of drinking water. I didn't believe they were out to kill me. I'll tell you—I was getting a kick out of it. A yarn as good as the pulps. I couldn't take it seriously. I suppose I wasn't using my head, but it seemed to me that I could reason with those fellows, especially if I were armed and they were at my mercy. You see? Naturally, I thought of my cabin. The ground around it was cleared, level, and that would give me the advantage. I imagined my stalkers trudging into the open to have their say. And all the while I'd keep them covered. Instead, I put myself squarely in a hole."

The two men who had stepped from the woods—one of them the now-deceased Souly—had called to Norton, who, with gun in hand, had half-emerged from his cabin.

"They didn't want to talk," proto-Norton ruefully explained. "They opened fire. Maybe I was expecting something like that. Anyway, I managed to dive back through the door."

"They thought you were me," I lied. It made more sense than telling him what was what.

In the course of events, this proto-Norton had lived, married, produced offspring. There was a chain here leading from him to Nina
and me. The bubble had thought us outside the chain, but he
hadn't been sure. This was no time to take chances. I said, "I'm not
going to tell you all of it. There're things it's better you don't know.
Let's say that I, and these people with me, work for the government.
Let's say we were investigating—"

"The bank," Glenway Norton broke in excitedly.

"That's right," I encouraged his error. "We were onto something
that certain parties didn't want uncovered. Apparently they found
out about us—about me, my name at least—and confused the pair
of us."

"What should I do?" Glenway Norton asked.

"Get out of town. This job will be done in a couple of weeks. Till
then you lay low."

He wouldn't hear of it—at first. Ten minutes of argument got us
only a maybe; another ten produced a possibly. By the time we were
hitting the home-stretch, Glenway Norton was willing to concede
that a short vacation might do him some good.

"One thing I don't understand," he said. "How you knew where
to look. No one knew about that cabin. It was a spot I'd kept from
all my friends. I had planned on a surprise unveiling."

It was time for one more piece of hokum. "The bureau which em-
ploys me has its ways," I said pompously. "We weren't entirely unaware of what was taking place."

*In my mind's eye I saw the map, each roadway, each path clearly
demarcated; I had gone over it a hundred times at least, for it spoke
of past glories and glory that was no more.*

*The cabin that had grown to a five-story mansion and finally be-
came an estate: the Norton estate. Built through labor, lost through
caprice in the shuffle of history. No one in our family could forget
the Norton estate. And as clan historian, I knew almost every inch
of it. As League historian, I'd had access to the old supplementary
maps.*

*This cabin would someday be Glenway Norton's second home.
And if a man isn't in his first home, you try his second.*

We let him off at Grand Central Station, forcing enough money on him—a loan, we called it—to keep him in style for a matter of weeks.

"Where should I go?" he asked.

"Anywhere. But make it far away."

Red neon lights spelled out: Katz's Delicatessen. Houston Street was still awake.

We turned down a side street, parked.

A narrow, littered hallway and two flights of uncertain stairs put us in our flat.

A single light had been left burning near the window. Long shadows sank into darker patches across the room.

Something stirred out of this darkness. By the easy chair in the far right corner, a man stood up. He was a medium-sized man in a long, belted trench coat. A wide, soft-brimmed hat dangled in his left hand from thumb and forefinger. He said, in a voice that was flat, expressionless:

"Which one of you is James Norton?"

FLEISHER NINE

"THAT'S THE BUNK"

James Norton, standing perfectly still, said, "I am."

"Uh-huh."

"And you, mister?"

"You should know me."

Norton moved a shoulder.

"My name's Eddy Fleisher."

Norton said, "How did you get in here?"

"The door. You figure I jimmy windows? Fire escapes give me the nosebleeds. I'm too old for stunts."

"The door was locked."

"Yeah. Believe me, you didn't want me camping in your hall."

"Berger send you?"

"Uh-uh. I sent me. Felix gave me the where. He says hello, by the way. DeKeepa was knocked-off last night, incidentally. Interested?"

Norton stared at Fleisher, saying nothing.

"Come on, folks. Take it easy. Take a load off your feet," Eddy Fleisher said cheerfully. "We got some goodies to chew over."

When they were all seated, Eddy Fleisher said, "Any luck with the Waller dame?" He said it as though expecting an answer. He got an answer.

"We haven't run into her," Norton said.

"She's around," Fleisher told him.

"You've seen her?" Nina said.

"Only her errand boys, lady."

"That sounds familiar," Brent said.

"I wouldn't mind," Fleisher told them, "getting my hands on her."

"Has she been giving you much trouble, Mr. Fleisher?" Nina asked.

"Much. Yeah, that's about the size of it. You know her, do you?"

"We have never had the pleasure," Brent said.

"She's only a name," Norton said. "Perhaps *you* can fill us in."

"I knew her," Fleisher said. "She was no one special. An exec—maybe that's special, huh? Not too many lady execs. Till she upped and powdered, it didn't mean a thing. Grace Waller: Fortyish. Married back in '18 to Donald R. Waller, a corporation counsel. Split some six years later. Amicable, as they say. Grace got herself a business degree from some college out West. Unusual? Maybe. Been with United Tool since '24. Working her way topside. Was holding down a more-or-less responsible slot when she dropped out. That's when I came into it, through the Kraft organization. Well, I'll tell you, Mr. Norton: folks take it on the heel and toe every day—get fed up with the grind, with the missus, with life itself, you know;

they just up and scram, and leave the other guy holding the bag. That's human nature, isn't it? What had the tool works in a lather was this: this Waller dame knew all kinds of hush-hush stuff; we figured maybe she'd sold out to the competition. That's not so unusual. Only nothing turned up. We figured something would show sooner or later, only it didn't. It still might, of course, but all this that's been happening points in another direction. I'll put it straight to you, Mr. Norton. When Berger first unloaded that spiel on me, I figured it for the bunk. I mean knocking off all those big-shots. What kind of a screwy deal was that? Only now I'm not so sure. Something's going on and the tool works is mixed up in it. Goren— a U.T. wheel—set me up for the kill this afternoon; can you beat that? Boris Goren! And the Waller dame showed in it, too. There's been too much blood in this thing. Berger's had half his shop cut from under him. DeKeepa's out. I see you're still kicking around, Mr. Norton, and I'm tickled pink. I figured you for next. You and me. Well, let me put it this way: I'm up to my neck in this now—in it, more or less, on my own hook, too. I aim to come out with a whole skin. Now, there're some points that have to be cleared up. Small points, but important. Like who are you? And how do you fit in all this? What's your angle? I've got to know, Mr. Norton, in order to protect myself. You see that, don't you? I don't think it's unreasonable. Not now, it isn't. Risks are pretty much part of this racket—that's okay—and I'm always ready to take a licking if the price is right—short of going under, that is. I draw the line there. You see what I mean? I've got to draw the line now. You've got to give me the lay. But listen—you play square with me, I'll come across with my end, with what I've got. Maybe the pair of us can crack this. We got a deal, Mr. Norton?"

Norton said, "It's true, Fleisher, you've gotten in pretty deep—"

"That's putting it mildly, brother."

"Berger tells me you're a traveling man."

"I get around, sure."

"That's your job . . ."

"Yeah. Part of it. I hit the Pullman plenty. So what?"

"This might be the right time to do some traveling," Norton said.

Eddy Fleisher smiled. "Forget that. I told you: too much has happened to too many. I'm in it—there's no helping that. I like being in it. It's not that simple, anyway. There's the folding stuff."

"Folding stuff?" Nina asked.

"Dough, lady. Where've you been all your life? The green's something I'm partial to."

James Norton said, "You'll have to be more specific, Fleisher. What've you got?"

"Sure. That's okay with me. That's fine. One of Berger's boys was a note fiend. Some ops save the shorthand for the wind-up spiel, but this Smiley got it all down as he went along. It takes all kinds, right? Only no one can find poor Smiley now. Berger and me, we figure he got hit with a lily—"

"What?" Nina said.

"Murdered, lady, croaked. You get that? He knew too much, that's what we figure. Berger had him on the Waller babe before she dusted. Smiley's notebooks turned up in Goren's safe. I've got them now. Interested? A little bit, huh?"

James Norton had reached a decision, said he was interested.

"I figured you might be," Eddy Fleisher said.

Norton nodded. "I'll tell you what I can." His voice sounded earnest.

"Yeah, you do that," Eddy Fleisher said.

"It's not much."

"I'll settle for what you give me—if it looks reasonable. But I won't buy a sucker's play. I'm too old and beat up for that."

"You won't have to. These two are my co-workers," Norton said. "You wouldn't have heard of me, of any of us, because that's how we wanted it. Let's just say I got a lot of money, all at once, and let it go at that. Some years ago. I could give you a date, a place, you might remember the event. I don't think that would help any of us. It'd be smoother to skip it. We're not in it anymore. We handle finance now."

"You bankroll what?"

"Things."

"But you don't lose by it?"

"No."

"The returns are okay, then?"

"Usually."

"The risk factor—?"

"Is considerable; higher than in your line."

"That's pretty high."

"Our associates," Norton said, "that's where we take our chances. You'd be surprised who we deal with."

"Not me."

"Anyway, about a year ago a piece of news came our way. It was about someone called Grace Waller, and it came from a reliable source—a business connection. Waller, it seemed, had entered our province, was staking some of the parties we'd backed from time to time. People come and go; there's money in it; but this, what they were going to do, was different—"

"Yeah, our mutual pal Berger, he spilled the beans about the *big kills*," Eddy Fleisher said. "He told me."

"We pieced it together. Our connection 'died' some three months later."

"So you started nosing around?"

"Not at once. We didn't take it that seriously. Things happened. We became interested."

"Yeah. I get that part of it, at least. But what beats me is your angle. What did you hope to get out of all this? You got to be fixed pretty good. Shakin' down the Waller dame—"

"That wouldn't be it."

"Okay—what was?"

"You know anything about Nazi Germany, Fleisher?"

"Yeah, I suppose so. I read the papers. What about it?"

"Want to live there?"

"You kiddin'?"

"How about Hitler?"

"A creeperoo."

"All right," James Norton said.

Eddy Fleisher laughed. "You trying to tell me, Mr. Norton, you took on this bunch because you don't like 'em?"

"Do you?"

Fleisher shrugged.

"I couldn't take what I had to the police."

"You're a patriot, Mr. Norton; you ought to put in for a medal."

"Of course. Only you'd have done the same."

"Uh-uh."

"No choice. Once *they* learned you were snooping. You see, I couldn't prove a thing—without getting tangled up in it myself, without bringing the law down on my own operation. I never planned it that way. The thing happened, that's all. I got sucked in. All right, two can play at that. I wasn't going to take it like some sitting duck. I've been around too long not to know what comes next. I went after Waller myself. I'm going to keep on after her. That's simple enough, isn't it? Well—that's all I can give you, that's all there is."

"Yeah," Eddy Fleisher said, "that's a crock of shit, all right." He held up a palm. "Save it. I can smell shit when I step in it. I expect to step in it. It's a nice yarn, though. I think you did real good, Mr. Norton. I admire your inventive abilities. And you're right about one thing. I *have* been sucked in. Here, lemme give you Joe Smiley's notebooks; maybe you can make something out of them—I can't."

NORTON TEN

THE BLOOD-LETTING

Two notebooks in all. I started flipping pages.

Eddy Fleisher put his hands in his coat pockets, stretched out his legs, and sank back into the easy chair.

Nina and Brent took turns looking over my shoulder. I don't know what they saw in it, what they made of the jottings.

Three table lamps now burned in our living room, giving off a dullish glow. Outside, darkness spilled over the streets like black ink out of a cracked bottle. It was as if our flat was a thing apart, severed from the rest of humanity.

Eddy Fleisher said, "I know this is pretty much of a long shot."

But Eddy Fleisher was wrong.

It would mean nothing to anyone of this day and age. Mere names. Names that would be so many worthless ciphers; a Manhattan phone book, in fact, would prove more enlightening.

But I knew.

Shelley Sypes was here.

Grace Waller had met twice with the diminutive Sypes in the ten days before her disappearance.

It would be five years before Sypes made his move. And even then few would know it. Historians of the future would ferret out his role in early 1940, painstakingly tracing the salesman's footsteps across Europe. Money would change hands on this trip, would ultimately find its way into the Soviet Union, into the pockets of Valodin, an obscure Russian infantry captain who, by assassinating Stalin, would pave the way for Gorchenkov's takeover—the one Russian who could do business with Hitler and preserve the Hitler-Stalin pact.

Simon Bevlin was here.

And six years from now, the retired storekeeper would run down Winston Churchill on a quiet side street in London.

Melinda Newberg was here.

She would fade from history, but not before introducing Grace Waller to Stephen Mallory. Mallory in turn would be Waller's connection with Vincent Lovelace. Lovelace—on April 18, 1941—would manage to cripple DeGaulle before being himself cut down. Charles DeGaulle would remain paralyzed, a bullet lodged in his spine. For him it would be all over.

Raymond McCloon.

Linda Summerwall.

Lansing Jeeter.

Marsha Billingsgate.

Bill Gorr . . .

Assassins, shadowy go-betweens, a man who knew a man who

knew a man. And to the eyes and ears of here-and-now, an invisible chain, one that could never be uncovered until long after the fact . . .

And here was one more name:

Joe Quartz.

Quartz was a locksmith. And Waller had had a key duplicated in his shop on a Tuesday morning three weeks ago. Before she vanished. What could be more innocent?

Joe Quartz.

Craftsman.

Joe Quartz.

Marksman.

Crazy Joe Quartz . . .

Who, in less than forty-eight hours, would make his first—unsuccessful—attempt on the life of President Franklin Delano Roosevelt.

And no one would be the wiser.

A gun jamming at the crucial moment, and Quartz would walk away from it all scot-free.

To try again. And succeed nine months later.

A footnote in a history text of the future. A single line, among hundreds, detailing other facts, places, dates in the life and times of Joe Quartz. Hero of the Annys. Murderer of Roosevelt. Initiator of the New Age.

For Roosevelt's demise brought down his party too. A coalition sued for peace on any terms. And the Americans-All Party picked up the pieces.

I had forgotten about Quartz, about that single line in a footnote which appeared in only one book.

For Grace Waller's name was never tied to Quartz in the "corrected" annals of the future. An ancestor of Lancaster, she was known for no specific deed, was only a name on a family tree.

But here she was.

And here was Joe Quartz.

Forty-eight hours away from his first try.

I put down the notebooks, turned to Eddy Fleisher.

"All right," I said.

"All right what?"

"Find me a Manhattan phone book," I said, "and I'll find you Grace Waller."

Essex Street was a clutter of ramshackle tenements, small shops, fire escapes. The *Jewish Daily Forward* building, a block away on East Broadway, loomed over the neighborhood like some benign giant, neon lights on its roof spelling out FORWARD in a lurid red.

It was three minutes past twelve.

Thursday, May 23, 1935.

The downstairs door wouldn't open.

Fleisher put his shoulder to it. It opened.

Wooden steps—too familiar by now—whose odors and curvature would remain with me always, led up toward the fourth floor. That was where we wanted to go.

No name was on the door at the top of the landing. Gold lettering, chipped and flaking, read: 4A.

The mailbox down below had offered a name to go with the lettering: Joe Quartz.

My gun was out, feeling wet and clammy in my hand, like a fish fresh out of the ocean.

Light shone under 4A. Voices came with it, murmuring.

Fleisher went against the door with a shoulder. The door popped open like a jack-in-the-box.

Four persons sat around a kitchen table. Through cigar and cigarette smoke I saw a woman, middle-aged, wearing pince-nez, with gray in her short, mannish hairdo. The face was familiar from official League and Incest portraits, and while they had gotten some of the features wrong, the essence had been captured.

Grace Waller.

And next to her, an even more familiar figure—if equally unprepossessing.

Eyes, heavy-lidded; nose, small and upturned; mouth, a cupid's bow. Seated now. Were he to rise, he'd stand four-foot-nine. Should he walk, it would be with a limp, his right leg twisted like crude strands of rope. Joe Quartz had reason to be bitter. He'd never know the adulation of future ages. His portrait, spread far and wide through all the Annys, was here in his own day confined to a few smudged snapshots.

The table crashed to the floor, spilling ashtrays, cigarette stubs, glasses and liquor bottles. Four hands reached for guns, four pairs of eyes peered at us through the thick smoke, showing fear, hate, panic.

The two unknowns were first. Professionals, they had moved with professional swiftness. Their hands groped for weapons.

But ours already held them.

Fleisher and I gunned them down.

The terror came then.

The scream.

We looked. We had to. Like automatons.

We turned our gaze to the upper left wall, and nothing on this earth could have kept us from doing that.

Dell Lancaster was there, *in the wall*. His chest, head, and arms sticking out of it like some crazed hunter's impossible trophy. His eyes were riveted on me, and he was screaming.

The laser he clutched fell from his waxen fingers. He clawed at the wall.

And died.

Behind us the stairs creaked.

Two very large guns in his small, shaking fists, a white-faced Boris Goren stepped through the still-open doorway, his eyes moving anxiously over the room. He saw the wall. His mouth opened slowly, like a frog sucking air; he swayed ever so slightly, as though about to take a low bow to some private—unheard—applause.

He didn't see the long shadow behind him on the stairs, was unaware of the man there who carefully raised and pointed his gun.

Felix Berger put a single bullet into the brain of Boris Goren.

Waller and Quartz moved. Not fast enough.

Three guns emptied themselves into their bodies.

From the flat across the hallway, sleepy-eyed Earl Kneely, clad in white striped pajamas resembling a prison uniform, shambled into our blood-letting.

"What've you done to my sister?" he demanded, aghast.

EPILOGUE

"You know," Eddy Fleisher said, "they never did find the legs, the torso."

"No, huh?"

"Uh-uh. They'd become part of the wall."

"Jesus."

"Yeah."

Both men were silent.

Eddy Fleisher said, "Some yarn, eh? You saw Lancaster in the wall, didn't you, Earl?"

Earl Kneely nodded, his face slack. "I saw him, all right." It was almost a whisper.

"I'll tell you," Eddy Fleisher said, "it made a believer out of me, damned if it didn't. That was the clincher."

"I guess it was. Hell, Eddy, put away the gat; you don't need that with me; you can have it back, the works, the haul, everything you and Kraft want; it's jake with me, Eddy . . ."

"That's not why. I told you all this for a reason, Kneely. You think this Lancaster ran the show?"

"Sure, why not, Eddy?"

"He didn't. That bunch took too many chances. You know how much they lost along the line? Norton says more than half were knocked off at one point or another. And that last stunt . . ."

Earl Kneely whispered, "How did it happen, Eddy? What was it?"

Fleisher shrugged. "Who knows? Norton was gumming their play. Someone had to be sent over to nix him, and Lancaster got the nod. Probably he used the same route as Norton and his pals: Lab Twenty-nine. Only they bungled it. A fluke. That time-viewer

dingus had too many bugs in it, kept clouding over. Norton Fifty-
nine got a lot of it cock-eyed himself. *And so did they."*

"Who's 'they,' Eddy?"

"The main ghees—the ones who called the turn—who sat back
living the life of Riley while Lancaster's crew got their brains beat
out running things. I'll tell you something else: odds have it those
chumps never even tumbled they were playing with a stacked deck.
So who had it real soft, Earl?"

Earl Kneely shrugged hopelessly.

"Father Pen," Eddy Fleisher grinned. "The cult keeper. And isn't
that something? *Incest.* The big taboo. Only here it gets the biggest
play of all. Because they needed it, couldn't do without it. That
time gizmo only worked for ancestors, for descendants. They could
only make contact with one of their own. The whole cult thing was
a blind for the Pen bunch, made what they were doing seem legit.
And all the while there was only one aim: it kept the wires open—
the *time wires,* Kneely. Without that, their set-up wouldn't've been
worth a plugged nickel."

Eddy Fleisher paused, went on:

"I'm just telling it like I got it from Norton. I'm not saying every
word is gospel. Some of it's just guesswork, the best we can do. You
know what's riding on all this—well, we figure we won. We're not
sure, but that's how it shapes up. Because proto-Pen is stretched out
on a slab now, and according to Norton Fifty-nine, *this* was the crucial time, the only time where it could all jell. And taking out proto-
Pen puts the skids under the whole operation."

Kneely licked his lips. "Who was he, Eddy?"

"Boris Goren. The ancestor. The first in line. Mousey Goren. But
that's who they had to deal with, and *through.* Only Goren could
catch their words, could receive the message. Norton Fifty-nine gave
us a bum steer about your sister, the Waller dame. Too many angles
couldn't be spotted through the viewer. Fifty-nine made a good
guess, all right; he fingered the Lancasters, but he was wrong. Lancaster's showing up here marks him and his line for stooges. The real
dynasty would never send one of their own: *it would've broken the
chain.* Goren had to be it. The Joe Smiley notebooks were stashed
in his safe. If Waller were king-pin, she'd never've turned them over

to Goren. Only the boss would rate goods that hot. Maybe Goren was waiting for some orders from above. Maybe it was just a slip-up. He hung on to the notebooks too long. The time-viewer was just out of whack, that's all. That's what tripped him up. Waller was heading the rub-out push, but Goren was the mouthpiece for the real engineer. He had to turn up at Quartz's. We put Felix Berger on Goren's tail last night and the old time-viewer never let out a squawk. A real blind spot."

Earl Kneely wiped sweat from his brow. "Who was running that other viewer, Eddy?"

Eddy Fleisher grinned. "Someone like old Fifty-nine, only further up the scale—that's the guess. So that Fifty-nine didn't even know about him. The last of the Pen line. Call him Super Pen; *his* viewer —unlike Norton's—could swap words with our time. More advanced. This Super Pen, it seems, was dishing out the know-how right down the line. That's how he kept his boys top-dog."

"This guy brought on all this grief?"

"Yeah. He engineered the break-ups, the future upheavals, planned them to a T. That's what Norton figures, anyway."

"Why, for chrissakes?"

"You've got me, pal. Maybe the end results of all that ruckus kept him sitting pretty up there. Maybe where he was—at his end of the line—he'd wound up some kind of World Emperor or something. Anyway, he fixed things for his crew—the ancestors—so they wouldn't kick; they went along with him no matter what, knowing they'd get by, be taken care of. They were sitting pretty, too. Each age had its secure, moneyed Pen, doing his *duty*, and looking out for the Incest Cult—promoting it—so that the DNA channels were kept tip-top."

Earl Kneely was shaking now. "Come on, Eddy, what's this got to do with me? What's the gun for, for chrissakes, Eddy—"

"Don't sweat it, Kneely. That's just so you'll remember real good later on."

"Later on?"

"Yeah. What I gave you looks like the goods, all right. It stacks up okay. But who can tell? Norton said I should have this chat with you. Goren was an orphan; he left no brothers or sisters. So maybe that's that. We hope so. But it could be we missed someone, a relative with the right DNA . . .

"Fifty-nine had a way of side-stepping history, some kind of a force-field or something. He'd live even if his ancestors didn't. Maybe this Super Pen has the same deal. They're both in the same league, aren't they? So just maybe he'll try to get his show back on the road. He'd want to come as close to the original scheme as he could. Your sister's gone, Kneely, but you're not. *And you'd make an okay stand-in.* That's what Norton wanted me to tell you."

"Jesus!"

"Norton wants you to know we'll be watching."

"I swear . . ." Kneely began.

"Norton figured you wouldn't want any part of a bum deal like that. And if someone ever braced you, you'd give us a call, real quick."

Kneely put a hand to his chest; his voice shook. "Cross my heart, Eddy . . ."

Eddy Fleisher lit a cigarette and slowly inhaled. He nodded once. "Sure," he said, "too many have bled."